# DUST CROWN

# Books by Kay L Moody

## Truth Seer Trilogy

## The Elements of Kamdaria

To receive special offers, bonus content, and info on new releases and other great reads, sign up for Kay L Moody's email list! You'll also get her short story collection for FREE.

**www.KayLMoody.com/gift**

Dust Crown
The Elements of Kamdaria 3
By Kay L Moody

Published by Marten Press
3731 W 10400 S, Ste 102 #205
South Jordan, UT 84009

www.MartenPress.com

Cover by Germancreative-fiverr
Edited by Deborah Spencer

ISBN: 978-16934230-0-0

The Elements of Kamdaria 3

# Dust Crown

## Kay L Moody

MARTEN
PRESS

# ONE

**THE EMPEROR'S MANSION HAD TO BE** defended with shaping.

Talise understood the plan when Commander Blaise explained it an hour ago. It all made sense on paper. A perfect strategy. She wasn't prepared for the way her heart pattered as she trudged across the palace gardens to the mansion.

*One step forward. Then another. Now step again and remember to breathe.*

She hadn't even looked at the emperor's mansion since arriving at the palace a few months ago. The lonely building stood on the opposite end of the garden from the palace. Its roof curved up at the ends just like all the buildings on the palace grounds. Unlike the palace's jade tiles, the emperor's mansion had charcoal tiles adorning the roof. For some reason, its presence seemed more terrifying than the army of Kessoku that would arrive soon.

She dug her fingernails into her palms, forcing herself to the present moment. *Not* an army.

Commander Blaise had explained it was just a *company* of soldiers. Two hundred fighters, and probably some of Kessoku's best, but not all of them. They knew Kessoku had at least a few thousand on their side.

A bitter taste entered her throat. Her muscles twitched as she remembered, yet again, how she had been lied to. Almost everyone in the palace had known Kessoku was out there, probably planning another attack. The emperor knew. Commander Blaise knew. General Gale. All the guards. The servants. Most of the court.

They all knew how dangerous Kessoku was, and not one single person had bothered to tell her or Aaden. Even Wendy had known. That cut Talise deeper than anything.

Wendy hadn't known everything, but she had picked up enough hints from General Gale that he swore her to secrecy.

Secrecy.

It didn't matter that the emperor had forbidden everyone from revealing information about the attack. No one could explain how Kessoku infiltrated the palace months ago, and all the Master Shapers and half the guards had been killed or taken prisoner. It didn't matter that the emperor threatened to execute anyone who let the truth slip.

What mattered was the emperor kept the secret from *her*. She and Aaden were the only two Master Shapers in all of Kamdaria. No wonder the emperor had chosen two Master Shapers. The palace had never needed them more desperately. And still, he didn't even trust them with the truth about their enemy.

That hurt.

The guards stopped short when they reached the chrysanthemum patch just outside the emperor's mansion. Nobody seemed to notice when Talise gasped at the sight of those flowers. Claye was still rubbing the sleep out of his eyes. Wendy whispered with the guards, probably going over the plan another time.

A warm set of fingers brushed against her elbow causing her to turn around. Without a word, Aaden stared into her eyes. He seemed to know instinctively how much anxiety was rushing through her.

*Of course* he did. Of course he was the only one who noticed her gasp. She tried to plaster a nervous smile on her face, but he seemed to know that was fake too.

He didn't say anything.

Neither did she.

They had both remained silent during the explanations and the planning. Perhaps he was just as frustrated as she was about being kept from the truth. It was all they could do to listen and nod and go along with the plan.

And they did have an important part in this plan.

"I see them." Wendy's whisper quivered through the air as she pointed. Following the finger, Talise saw ten heads pop over a ridge. One of the many advantages to the location of Ridgerock Palace was the fact that it had been built on a mountain. Already, Kessoku had used a great deal of energy just climbing the steep rock that led them to the palace grounds.

What type of weapons would they have? Perhaps it was a strange thought to have, but there it was anyway. They knew Kessoku's base was in the Gate, the middle ring of Kamdaria. That meant they didn't have access to the same resources or artisans as the elite had in the Crown. But, if any members of Kessoku had a silver crescent moon on their ID card, they could easily purchase excellent weaponry in the Crown, and have it delivered to the Gate.

At least none of the fighters would be from the Storm. A shiver shook through Talise's shoulders as she recalled her former home. Though weak and desperate, no one fought more fiercely than those who lived in the outer ring of Kamdaria. She had once seen a man keep fighting even after he had one arm sliced clean off. Even with weakened bodies and no shaping, no one could match the ferocity found in the Storm. Because in the Storm, people had nothing left to lose.

With a small glance at Aaden, they both raised their hands and started shaping.

As discussed, they began by shaping the water out of the stream that ran through the garden. They levitated the water through the air and sent it splashing down on Kessoku like a waterfall. When the water hit the men with its full force, they levitated it back up and sent it crashing down again. Over and over.

She didn't look closely enough to know if any Kessoku lost their grip and fell because of the water. A part of her didn't want to know.

Their shouts were unintelligible from so far away, but they *were* shouting. Each time the water crashed down on them, the shouting became more distressed.

Stage one of their plan was a success. As they had suspected, Kessoku never expected to be attacked with shaping. Since the other Master Shapers were dead, they must have assumed the palace soldiers would rely on swords and arrows.

The water didn't stop them for long. Luckily, their plan never expected it to.

She and Aaden glanced at each other again. He dropped his hands to prepare for the next stage. Fist-sized rocks began levitating off the ground as Aaden used earth shaping to drop them into a pile at their sides.

The moment he stopped shaping, she felt the absence of his power. He had shaped so much water and made it look effortless.

She continued levitating the water and making it crash down. She tried to lift as much as they had done together, but it was more difficult than she expected.

At least twenty Kessoku soldiers cleared the ridge now and moved past her waterfall. They ignored the emperor's mansion completely and marched toward the palace. Gritting her teeth together, Talise shaped a wall of water about ten feet in front of them. They laughed at the barrier and kept marching without missing a beat.

She felt the eyes of the palace soldiers on her, watching, waiting for her to make the next move. But she ignored them. No Kessoku had ever seen what she was about to do, and she planned to fully exploit the element of surprise.

As the Kessoku soldiers marched on, their expressions hardened. It wasn't until the first row of soldiers made contact with the wall of water that she began to act again.

Fire flooded through her veins as she froze her hand and arms all the way up to her elbows. She pushed her hands through the air to send a chill to the wall of water.

Just as the Kessoku soldiers began sticking their toes and hands through the water in a march, it crystalized into a wall of ice.

Even through the ice, she saw how every jaw of the Kessoku soldiers had dropped. When they tried to free their feet from the ice, it held firm.

Stage two. Success.

Talise gulped as more Kessoku climbed over the ridge. There were at least fifty of them now. Their momentary surprise at seeing ice shaping had already vanished. Using the hilts of their swords, plus a bit of fire shaping, they tore the ice wall down.

She shaped it back up again each time, but they were getting faster. She wouldn't be able to hold them with the ice wall forever.

Behind her, the others were getting into position. Two rows of guards stood in front of the mansion, holding a sword in one hand and a spear in the other. Wendy and Claye stood among them. Aaden took his place at her side.

Her heart rate increased as Kessoku broke down her wall again. The time drew near for the next stage of the plan. Even after years of training on focus and restraint, nothing could prepare her for this.

A real enemy marched a garden's length away. No matter how good her shaping, one wrong move could lead to death at their hands.

Gulping again, she raised her hands and gave a nod to Aaden.

Time to fight.

# TWO

**THE ICE WALL HAD BEEN FORGOTTEN.**
Kessoku stomped over the ice fragments with the same determination they wore while climbing over the ridge. In the violet hue of sunrise, they stomped, looking ready to kill.

Guilt washed over Talise as they drew closer. The dilemma had roiled through her mind at least a dozen times already. She wasn't a killer. She didn't want their blood on her hands. She didn't want any blood on her hands.

But this was a war. One that Kessoku had started.

An urge to fight hardened inside her. The feeling was almost opposite to when she'd been safe in the strategy room with Commander Blaise making these plans. In her head, she didn't believe she could ever kill anyone.

But out here, it was different. Each member of Kessoku had murder in their eyes. It was obvious they meant to destroy any obstacle between them and the emperor without regard for life.

In this moment, she finally understood the words Commander Blaise had spoken an hour before. "Don't think of it as killing the enemy. Think of it as defending Kamdaria."

The distinction didn't seem significant in the strategy room. But with their weapons glinting in the sun, it made sense now.

It was her life or theirs. They were the ones who made the rules, but she still had to play by them. She wasn't about to die now.

Clenching her jaw, she levitated a handful of the rocks off the pile Aaden had made earlier. Once in the air, she shaped the rocks across the garden until they slammed against the faces of the Kessoku soldiers marching toward her.

Her first wave of rocks drew blood from at least five of them. One Kessoku soldier used the bottom of his tunic to wipe the sticky liquid dripping from his forehead. Another soldier spit out a broken tooth. Even after her attack, none of them showed the slightest sign of giving up.

Shaping more rocks from the pile, she began again. Aaden sent rocks toward them as she did, but then he added a new strategy. He shaped a small mound of earth in front of a soldier just as the soldier began to step forward. The solider immediately tripped over the earth mound. He took another soldier down as he tried to regain his balance.

Talise used Aaden's technique, and soon soldiers were tripping in every direction.

Anger twitched at the muscles around their mouths. They glared at the earth as if angry something so simple impeded their progress. Soon, the soldiers lifted their knees to their chests with each step, and the earth could trip them no more.

Talise shaped more rocks, sending them straight for their skulls. Though the rocks drew blood, they never hit hard enough to knock anyone out. Perhaps her shaping wasn't strong enough. Or perhaps she didn't have it in her to kill.

Despite that, Kessoku did get injured. The effects were more psychological, but that was a win. When Kessoku came to the palace months ago, they breached the palace without anyone realizing until it was too late.

Now they were met with painful resistance, and they hadn't even gotten past to the garden. Their boots stomped through the mud with clear determination, but Talise could see their steps were more measured than before. It gave her a wave of hope. Maybe they'd leave if they realized what they were up against.

She shaped a rock from the pile. Eyeing the soldiers who wore Kessoku's patch of three interlocking circles over their hearts, she chose the weakest looking one. Her rock arched over the garden before she slammed it into the soldier's stomach with as much force as possible. This time, she didn't hold back. Shaping all her strength into the rock made a much bigger impact than her other attacks had.

The Kessoku soldier dropped to her knees. She clutched her stomach with a grunt. A moment later, she fell onto her back passed out cold.

Talise allowed herself to accept the victory. She still couldn't bring herself to hit the soldiers in the head, but this was close enough. She had dropped the soldier, hadn't she?

Aaden seemed to like her idea. He began shaping rocks into the stomachs of more Kessoku soldiers. Soon, a line of them lay on the ground. The ones behind had to climb over their fellow soldiers before they could continue down the path.

"Stop it," one of the palace guards hissed in her ear.

She turned around with a start, surprised to see the guard so close. He must have come away from his spot by the emperor's mansion just to talk to her.

The guard had a thick, spidery scar on his chin and a silver hooped earring in one ear. His eyebrows furrowed. "If you don't have the stomach to kill them, then let someone else do it. Knocking them out does us no good."

Aaden nodded and went back to throwing his rocks at the Kessoku's heads and shoulders.

Talise gave a short nod to the guard with the spidery scar, but her stomach twisted as she turned back to the fight. The plan had been simple. Defend the emperor's mansion with shaping. Make Kessoku think this was the real fight.

And then fail.

That was the most important part. They had to give Kessoku an early victory, so their enemy would be overly confident when the real fight began. Then, when the palace army took over, Kessoku wouldn't know what hit them.

That part of the plan didn't allow for members of Kessoku to be knocked out or taken prisoner. All of them were supposed to be killed. Talise gulped and tried to distract her mind by shaping.

At least the killing part wasn't her responsibility.

A clump of rocks flew at her command, but it lacked the necessary force to truly injure anyone.

Yes, the Kessoku soldiers had to die, but she didn't want to be the one to do it.

Her heart squeezed as she shaped more rocks from the pile. She tried to convince herself to hit harder, but the conviction for it was buried deep underneath the fresh grief of Marmie's death.

When she shaped another wave of rocks, they didn't reach their targets. Instead, a wave of air made them bounce to the ground. Finally, Kessoku had decided to use more shaping against them.

Before she could think of a counterattack, a Kessoku man on the edge of their ranks lifted his sword and let out a loud cry. The rest of Kessoku yelled with him as they began charging the emperor's mansion.

They didn't just march, they ran. Talise took a step back. The Kessoku had already closed half the distance between them. Her stomach lurched. It was time to enact the next part of their plan.

"Raise your spears!" Talise shouted.

Aaden grabbed her wrist and pulled her to safety behind the two rows of palace guards. She didn't bother pulling her hand out of his grip or telling him how unnecessary it had been. There was no time.

Once behind the palace guards, Aaden dropped her wrist and immediately raised his hands to shape. Talise joined him and together they shaped a wall of air that would push Kessoku away from them.

"We need more air!" Wendy shouted. She stood just in front of Talise with her spear pointed toward the Kessoku.

Talise shaped harder, letting the width of the air wall grow thicker. Next to her, Aaden shaped so hard, the muscles in his forehead twitched.

At last, Kessoku reached the air wall that separated them from the palace guards. Without any hesitation, they pressed forward through the air.

Talise shaped harder. She could feel Kessoku stepping through the wind as she and Aaden shaped it. It took effort for them just to move each foot forward. They had to shove against the wind, fighting through it with as much effort as it took to move a boulder.

Talise held her breath.

She couldn't help it. Their swords were so close, she was certain something would make it through the wall of wind.

A breath rattled through her as she gritted her teeth together. With a new resolve, she shaped even harder, knowing this would only make Kessoku push harder as well.

In front of her, Wendy pointed her spear forward. Her knuckles had turned white from the death grip she maintained.

Since their lives were on the line, now probably wasn't the best time to be angry at Wendy. Yet, a rush of resentment trickled up through Talise's toes anyway. Wendy had lied to her. Her *best friend* had lied to her. Considering the circumstances, Talise had no right to be upset about it. She knew that. But it was surprisingly difficult to let it go.

If she and Aaden had known Kessoku was coming, they might have been better prepared. They might have been able to do more than just pretend to defend the emperor's mansion with shaping.

Wendy raised one fist into the air, and Talise sucked in a breath. She glanced at Aaden. He had one eye on her and one on Wendy's fist.

Talise tried to ignore Aaden, which was also surprisingly difficult. She narrowed her eyes at Wendy's fist, waiting for the signal.

Kessoku pressed forward.

Closer.

Still Wendy's fist hung high in the air.

When Talise could make out the freckles on a Kessoku man's face, her breath hitched. They were too close. Her hands shook, which sent a vibration through her perfect wall of wind. Her eyes narrowed again. She *needed* to focus.

But they were right in front of her. A whole row of Kessoku marched into the wind, their swords raised. One wrong move and those swords would run through the palace guards. Once they were gone, they'd move on to the next row of guards.

Wendy's fist was still raised. Talise curled her toes and held her breath.

Waiting.

Finally, when the Kessoku were only a few steps from the guards' spears, Wendy's fist dropped. On cue, Talise and Aaden shaped away the wall of wind.

With the sudden absence of resistance from the wind, every member of Kessoku stumbled forward. They were unable to catch their balance until... they landed on the spears of the palace guards.

Talise grabbed Aaden's arm as she watched the life go out of a woman's eyes. She gulped.

This was real now.

"Charge!" a Kessoku man called from behind the others. Talise tripped over her feet as she tried to back away. There were too many of them. The wind trick had only killed a handful of Kessoku, and the rest barreled forward.

The death of their fellow men had barely given Kessoku any pause. They climbed over the fallen soldiers as if they were earth and rock, not people they knew. And now they moved toward Talise and the others looking eager to kill.

There was no chance in fighting anymore. Kessoku would win. Their swords and spears glinted in the morning sun.

"Run!" Aaden shouted.

He'd been pulling her along, but somehow, they had gotten separated in the chaos. Talise lunged over a nearby bush to avoid the point of a sword. She was back up a moment later, ignoring how her hands stung from the recent fall. Her feet found every branch and bush as she sprinted through the garden. With each step, she could practically feel Kessoku's swords straining to reach her neck.

She had to remind herself this was part of the plan too. They were *supposed* to retreat. They were supposed to make Kessoku think they had won an early victory. But it didn't feel like things were going according to plan. It felt like Kessoku was right on her heels, and she was about to die.

The world seemed like a fog of gray around her. The Kessoku were behind her, she knew that for sure, but the palace guards could have been anywhere. She was vaguely aware that Aaden's arm was tight in her grip, but she couldn't remember when she had caught back up to him. Her fingernails were probably digging into his skin, though he said nothing about it.

When Wendy tripped on a nearby rock, Talise gasped and fell to a halt. Fear gripped her as she helped Wendy to her feet. A dagger whistled past her ear.

Aaden was pulling her now. And she was pulling Wendy.

In that moment, her sense of direction evaporated completely. Were they still by the emperor's mansion? Had any of the palace guards been injured? And Claye.

Panic ripped through her insides, causing her to grip Aaden harder.

Where was Claye?

"Over here! Hurry!" Claye's whispered voice was a relief amidst the chaos. At the sound of it, Talise found her feet and began running with a renewed sense of direction.

She ducked through a dense bush and then shaped a clump of earth toward her pursuers. Aaden threw fire balls over his shoulder, which pushed back a few Kessoku.

They entered the hedge maze from their trials and lost the rest of Kessoku through there. When they exited the maze through a brand new opening, Talise rushed for the foxhole where they were meant to hide.

Her breath came in sharp pants as she scanned her new surroundings. How many of them had made it?

# THREE

**TALISE PRESSED HER PALM AGAINST** the wet earth of the foxhole, hoping it would ground her. She tried to take steadying breaths, but with each inhale her lungs shuddered. *Relax,* she told herself. *We made it.*

She finally admitted to herself the real reason she was afraid to look around. *Had* they made it? All of them?

She let out a breath of relief when she saw Wendy, hand over her heart, sucking in air like it was her first time breathing.

Aaden stood nearby. His forearm was red where she had been gripping it, but at least her fingernails hadn't dug deep enough to draw blood. He glanced over the foxhole, out of breath but still on alert.

The palace guards were there too. Eleven of them. Was that all? She hadn't counted them before, but shouldn't there have been an even number? That thought was interrupted by an even more pressing one.

Where was Claye?

Gripping her stomach, she jerked her head side to side. No, Claye had to be there. He had just told them to hurry. He *had* to be there.

"We deserve a medal for this." The voice was low enough that Kessoku wouldn't hear, but it was Claye's.

Her head zipped toward him. He stood behind a few of the palace guards, almost out of view. He was bent at the waist, gripping his side like his guts would spill out if he let go. He sucked in a huge breath then let out an even bigger one. "I thought gardening was murder, but this?" He shook his head while a solemn resignation filled his eyes. "Look at this injury."

Her heart stopped. *What injury?* Claye was panting heavier than any of them. And the way he gripped his side...

But when Claye lifted his arm, he displayed his hand with a short scratch on the back. He'd probably gotten it from a tree branch.

Talise heaved a sigh of relief as she rested her forehead on the soil of the foxhole.

Wendy had her hand over her mouth, eyes as wide as lemons. She blinked several times before she moved again. When she did, she curled her hands into fists and began jabbing every inch of Claye with soft thuds. "You absolute *vermin*!" she whispered. "How could you scare me like that?" She pounded on his arms even as he tried to get away. "That was not funny!"

A breath of relief came out with the chuckle that escaped Talise's lips. Even if it was small, it felt good to laugh.

When Aaden glanced over the foxhole again, Talise decided to join him. "Can you see the palace from here?" she asked.

He jerked his head to the left, pointing toward the palace grounds with his chin. Following his line of sight, she peered between two bushes and finally saw Kessoku. They weren't far from the main palace, but a small group of them hung back.

The small group stood around the emperor's mansion doing something with their hands. A moment later, they let out war cries as the wooden walls of the mansion burst into flames. The sight of it made her stomach clench.

The mansion wouldn't be missed. No one used it now that Emperor Flarius refused to enter its walls. Commander Blaise had made sure the mansion was empty before Kessoku arrived.

Still, seeing it on fire made Talise think of all those years ago when Kessoku had attacked the first time. They had killed the emperor's family, only missing the emperor through a small miracle. The flames felt like a message. This time, they were back to finish the job.

She pulled her eyes away from the mansion and directed her attention back to the rest of Kessoku. No one would miss the mansion anyway, what did it matter if it burned? A tiny knot in her stomach reminded her of the sweet smell those chrysanthemums made. Maybe those would be missed.

The faces of the Kessoku were hard to see as they stormed through the gardens on their way to the main palace. The Kessoku had given up trying to find them. They seemed to think it would be easy to enter the palace.

When they had first been attacked with shaping, they almost seemed dejected. First the waterfall, then the ice wall, then the rocks slamming into their faces. The psychological warfare had been as effective as they intended.

But none of them seemed the least bit frightened now. Even after several of their men had died on the palace guards' spears, they looked as eager as ever. Confident.

*Good.* That was exactly what they hoped for. Make Kessoku think they had earned a great victory. Build them up just to crash them down.

Perhaps the victory would have tasted sweeter if there were something to watch. Talise narrowed her eyes at the Kessoku soldiers. Ignoring the shiver that threatened to pass through her, she said, "Shouldn't General Gale's men be shooting arrows by now?"

No one responded.

Talise glanced back at Wendy, but her friend only shrugged. Despite the lack of words, the crease between Wendy's eyebrows spoke volumes.

Had something gone wrong? Had Kessoku found a way into the palace after all?

The emperor's mansion, that was nothing. Unimportant. But if Kessoku had already breached the palace, they were definitely in trouble. No matter how much the emperor criticized Talise, she knew he couldn't die. Kamdaria needed him.

Her gut twisted around and around. Everyone else seemed tense, but no one seemed nearly as anxious as her. Why wasn't anyone doing anything?

She pulled herself up out the foxhole to get a closer look through the branches of a hedge bush.

The Kessoku weren't running toward the palace anymore. They were regrouping.

They still had an entire garden to march through before they reached the palace walls. Still, they were closer than they should have been, and Talise couldn't take it anymore.

She inched back down to the foxhole and faced the others. "We have to do something. No one from the palace is attacking. Kessoku is regrouping. They're going to start marching soon, and we can't let them get to the palace."

The twisting in her gut didn't ease when she noticed one of the guards rolling his eyes and another scoffing at her words.

She gritted her teeth. Maybe they didn't like her idea, but they were just guards. She bore the title of Master Shaper, which gave her authority. They'd have to learn to respect that. Lifting her chin, she said, "I need five guards to use dirt and leaves to disguise themselves. Those guards will distract Kessoku by slipping through the trees unnoticed until they attack on my command. They'll never see it coming. When those five guards have all been killed, the rest of us will start to attack from here."

The guard that had scoffed earlier shifted on his feet until he faced Talise. "Are you insane?"

The words cut through her, making her feel as incompetent as she had after the maze trial. After setting her jaw, she said, "It's a good strategy."

Now the guard laughed and slapped a nearby guard with a friendly pat. "Oh, of course, *strategy*. That's all that matters."

Talise dug her toe into the ground. Her shoulders tensed but she managed to keep them from bunching up. The image of the burning mansion came to her mind, along with the Kessoku who had been impaled by spears. "What could be more important than strategy at a time like this?"

The palace guard blinked in return. Maybe he expected her to know what was going on in his head, but she didn't. When he seemed to sense her confusion, the guard let out a huff. His fingers curled into a fist, which matched the vein pulsing in his forehead. His demeanor held so much rage, it almost frightened her.

"I think food could be more important. It's always a good time for food." Claye attempted a smile, but Wendy only shushed him.

The air around them turned thick as the soldiers glared at Talise. They were all as angry as the one who argued against her. Finally, the first guard gestured to the men behind him. "These are people, not Forces tablets. Your so-called *strategy* involves five people sacrificing their lives just to create a diversion." He took a step back and all the guards around him stood tall, sneering at Talise. "People. People are more important than strategy."

A lump hardened in Talise's throat. She let the words pierce through her and sting. She deserved it.

It didn't matter that she'd been trying to save everyone in the palace. The guard was right. Strategy on a Forces board would never be the same as strategy on a real battlefield. Because a battlefield used real people.

She had no time to let these thoughts sink in. Kessoku had just finished regrouping and were now ready to march again.

"Look." Aaden had come to her side. It seemed to be his favorite place now that the trials were over. He pointed up at the palace roof. The jade tiles looked the same as they always did, which she was about to point out.

But then she noticed movement in the tiny slits of windows just under the roof. Glinting in the morning sun, the tips of several arrows sat just under the jade roof tiles. Her breath relaxed. The shooters were there. Ready.

Her heart thumped in her chest as she waited. And waited.

# FOUR

**ONE HUNDRED SEVENTY-EIGHT** Kessoku soldiers marched toward the palace. Once Talise had counted them all, she finally realized what the palace army had been waiting for. The Kessoku were all there now. None of them was still climbing the ridge that led to the palace. Now they all stood in the palace garden, ready to be slaughtered.

Talise climbed out of the foxhole and crept closer to the march. She wasn't supposed to fight, but she couldn't bear sitting back and doing nothing. At the very least, she wanted to see everything as it happened.

Aaden and Wendy joined her but not Claye. The three of them crawled behind a large hedge bush where they could see everything without being in danger.

Kessoku marched forward and soon hit the natural barriers the garden provided. The large hedges forced Kessoku into a funnel shape, one that got smaller the closer they got to the palace.

Breathing became a forced task instead of something natural. Kessoku looked even stronger than before. They marched with an air of invincibility, probably because of their recent victory.

*Why wasn't the palace army attacking?*

Just as that thought entered her mind, the arrows began showering down. One fourth of the Kessoku soldiers fell in that first wave. They dropped to the ground while the others scrambled to climb over them. Another wave of arrows fell and even more Kessoku dropped.

Now that the arrows had started to fall, Kessoku figured out where they were coming from. They shot their own arrows toward the tiny windows just under the palace roof.

When cries of pain erupted from the windows, Talise knew some of the Kessoku arrows met their marks. Her insides writhed, filling her with the need to act.

Commander Blaise had made it painfully clear they weren't supposed to engage Kessoku in any way once they had left the emperor's mansion.

But she couldn't just stand here and watch. Not with the palace under attack. Lifting a hand, she began shaping dirt from the ground.

"What are you doing?" Aaden stared at her hands as he spoke.

She kept her eyes on the dirt and continued shaping. "I did this against those other Kessoku in the training room. I'm going to shape dirt and air together into a dirt cloud. Then Kessoku won't be able to see well enough to shoot arrows into the palace."

Without another word, Aaden began shaping his own clumps of dirt in the air.

Wendy squeezed Talise's shoulder and shook her head so hard her black hair skittered across her shoulders. Though her voice was timid, the words were clear. "You can't do that. If you cover Kessoku with a dirt cloud, the palace soldiers won't be able to see them either. They need to see Kessoku in order to aim."

Talise bit into her bottom lip as she nodded. Wendy was right. The dirt clouds would confuse Kessoku, but it would probably give them more of an advantage than anything. She needed something that would help the palace soldiers and hurt Kessoku.

Perhaps she could throw rocks at their hands so they couldn't fight. Or maybe she could try tripping them again.

When she dismissed those thoughts, she noticed Aaden staring at her. He focused on her face, but the wheels in his head seemed to be turning too. "What if we make the dust clouds cover their faces, but not their heads?"

A bubble of excitement filled Talise. She clapped her hands together and leaned toward him feeling an almost smile on her face. "Yes. We'll make the dust cloud cover them from the crown of their head and down. Then the palace soldiers will still be able to see the crowns of their heads, but Kessoku won't be able to see the palace."

Wendy opened her mouth to say something, but Talise and Aaden were already busy shaping the dust clouds. Instead of speaking, Wendy had apparently decided to help.

Wendy chewed her bottom lip as she shaped wind through a dirt clod. The dirt burst open to a cloud of dust, but it fell to the ground a moment later.

Talise could see her friend struggling to shape both air and earth at the same time. She almost offered to do the dust part so Wendy wouldn't have to fail. But Wendy seemed intent on shaping the two elements, no matter how hard it was.

That made it a little easier to forget the anger she still harbored for her friend. It was times like this Talise remembered Wendy hadn't made it to the elite academy because of her sweet smile. Wendy's skill didn't match Talise's or Aaden's, but her shaping was still far better than most Kamdarians.

When the three of them had produced a large enough dust cloud, they carefully shaped it into the crowd of Kessoku. The soldiers began swatting the air, trying to clear the dust away.

Talise stepped closer. The dust had to cover the Kessoku's eyes but not their heads. The balance had to be just right. Soon, the palace soldiers began picking off the Kessoku soldiers like they were the single cherry in a bucket of blueberries.

The arrows soared. Talise kept shaping.

Minutes passed. Then even more passed. Then even more.

It felt like hours since the fight had begun. Maybe it had been.

Wendy's breathing became shallow. Finally, she dropped her arms to massage her muscles. Watching it made Talise's muscles feel like fire. A growing fire.

With a bout of determination, Talise sent a fresh wave of dust through the Kessoku. The effort cost her. Her arms shook with the effort of keeping them in the air.

After a quick glance at the sky, it became clear a few hours had indeed passed. The sun had cleared the sunrise stage and was climbing in the sky. If it were a regular day, she and Aaden would have been training for several hours already. It all came back to her then.

She remembered how she had stayed up late the night before throwing daggers with Wendy. Then she had been woken up long before dawn to capture the Kessoku scout group with Aaden. Now it was several hours past dawn, and her arms and body could take the stress no more.

One glance at Aaden told her his body fought for strength the same way hers did.

She let her arms drop to her sides.

With her weakened muscles, there was nothing else to do. She had done everything she could. It was up to the palace soldiers now.

Aaden also let his arms drop. Within seconds, the dust cloud cleared. A hollow grief took hold of Talise's stomach. Kessoku soldiers were still there, fighting to reach the palace.

But so many more were dead.

The ground was littered with their bloody bodies. Muddy footprints covered many of the fallen soldiers' tunics. Limbs were twisted at strange angles. A wave of nausea shot through Talise.

She did this.

She hadn't shot the arrows that killed them, but her shaping had helped. And now they were dead.

Without thinking, she grabbed onto Wendy and Aaden. A lump lodged in her throat, making it hard to swallow. She didn't see the soldiers who were steps away from the palace walls. She only saw the wave of destruction before her.

There were only about thirty Kessoku soldiers left. They charged the palace, letting out loud war cries. They tried to ignore their fallen friends, but it was difficult to do so when they kept tripping over them.

Their final steps to the palace were made into a funnel with large hedges. Smoke billowed above the hedges, but they must have been shaped with extra water in the leaves because the hedges seemed unable to burn with fire shaping. The Kessoku were forced to charge the palace in the tight funnel. By the time they got there, they could stand in rows no wider than two by two.

All at once, the palace doors swung open, revealing a squad of palace soldiers with swords in their hands. They cut down the Kessoku before them without a trace of exhaustion. The palace soldiers had the clear advantage. These were obviously fresh soldiers who had been able to rest recently. They also had many soldiers to fight against the few Kessoku that could make it through the tight funnel. Behind the palace soldiers, even more soldiers stood on tables and shot arrows at the remaining Kessoku.

Talise's gut twisted at the destruction. The palace soldiers cut down one Kessoku after another. Though she was glad to see the palace soldiers winning, she was conflicted at witnessing so much death. Even if they were the enemy, these people must have had families. And those families would soon be grieving.

Without warning, Aaden jumped through the bush and closer to the palace. Before he could run off, Talise scrambled over to his side. "What are you doing?" she asked, even as he jogged toward the destruction.

He scanned the ground, staring closely at the dead men. "I'm checking for survivors. Some of them might have passed out from blood loss but aren't actually dead."

A reminder in her head told her Commander Blaise—not to mention the emperor—wouldn't approve of her getting so close to the battle. But she couldn't stand around waiting anymore.

Splitting up, she and Aaden took careful steps through the carnage. She placed her fingers on the necks of every fallen soldier to check for a pulse. Each time her fingers were met with cold stillness.

These were people littering the ground, but in her head, all she could see were rows and rows of unmarked graves. Then she started thinking of silly things. Would the palace return the bodies to their families? Would the Kessoku even ask to have the bodies returned? How were dead bodies transferred? How much would it smell?

"Over here!" Aaden's voice carried over the shouts and clinks of swords that still came from the palace doors. Talise scurried to his side.

He had found a still-breathing soldier, but this was one of their own men. A palace guard who had been with them at the emperor's mansion. The spidery scar on his chin looked as pale as the rest of his face. With a growing panic, Talise tore the man's shirt collar down to search for the injury that had knocked him out.

Aaden grabbed her hands with a gentleness she didn't expect. He pointed to the back of the man's head. A large gash had blood pouring from it, but just under the blood, she could make out a cracked skull.

Her hands flew to her mouth as she sucked in a gasp. This man was a living ghost. When he let out a groan, her heart nearly stopped. He blinked and reached for his head.

She didn't know much about healing, but seeing that wound, she didn't think it would help if the man touched it. Instead, she took the man's hand in hers and said, "Try to relax."

The man balked at the sight of her. He squirmed, pushing her away as his jaw worked up and down. Then, he moaned when his head seemed to proclaim its pain.

"It's okay," she said. "Don't move."

But her words only distressed him more. He opened his mouth but couldn't seem to find any words. He looked her straight in the eye and let out a groan that made her feel like she should have left him alone.

And then everything changed again. His eyes slid to the back of his head, so only the whites were visible. His muscles went rigid and then they started shaking. She grabbed his hand, trying desperately to stop whatever was happening.

The healers were skilled. They must have had a way to fix this. But the man only shook harder. She couldn't shake the feeling that this was the end. Why did she have to be here to see it? Heat roiled with sadness went slicing through her.

She turned to Aaden, desperate for help, but he looked as much at a loss as she felt. "Do something," she said while clutching the guard's hand.

Aaden only swallowed and looked away. "I don't know how."

Her heart pounded in her chest. She knew he couldn't know what to do. She didn't know either, but that didn't take away the bitterness of battle. They had found a survivor. And it had come to nothing.

The guard's throat gurgled as he tried to speak. He let out a cough which sent blood spattering everywhere. And then, everything stopped. His body relaxed, the shaking gone. His eyes fluttered closed.

In his final breath, he uttered one word. "Aria."

And then he was gone. The lump in Talise's throat grew so large she could barely breathe. Tears stung in her eyes before they fell in thick drops from her lashes. She wanted to scream. She wanted to reach for Aaden. She wanted to close her eyes and wake up from this nightmare.

Before she could act on any of those things, a movement from behind made her turn.

"Watch out!" Aaden shouted, but it was far too late.

A sword was crashing down, ready to strike her skull. Her body reacted before her mind had even processed the moment. She sent a blast of fire at her attacker's face. He cried out and took a step back. But then he swung his blade again.

The tip of it brushed across her shoulder. It pierced her skin, though the muscle seemed untouched. He swung again, and Aaden was there. Talise shaped a wave of wind to help, but then she tripped, and it did nothing.

Everything was a jumble of limbs and dust. She wanted to send another burst of fire, but she didn't want it to hit Aaden. She reached through the air, clawing at the arms that seemed eager to harm her.

Aaden cried out and then another voice came. The Kessoku solider. She was lying on the ground, her face pressed into the soil. A heavy boot sank into her back, crushing the spine. She tried to crane her neck back, but all she saw was the glint of a sword in the sunlight.

And then Aaden fell to the ground with a grunt. The sword came swooshing down over him, and everything seemed to move in slow motion.

Talise shoved the boot off her back and sent a burst of fire at the Kessoku soldier. His sword faltered at the sight of the flames but not enough.

The sword kept falling. Talise could see he intended to strike both her and Aaden in one blow. She prepared to shove her boots against his ankles, hoping to trip him and make his grip on the sword falter.

Before her feet could reach their target, an arrow sliced through the air, piercing the soldier in the heart. She screamed as his body, not just his sword, fell toward her. She barely had a moment to breathe before his body crushed hers to the ground.

The sense of suffocation overtook her, but it seemed completely insignificant when Aaden's strangled cry cut through the air. She barely had the strength to push the dead soldier off her.

When she did, she saw Aaden throwing the soldier's sword off his chest before he buried his face in his hands. She moved toward him, but he jerked away.

She probably would have given him space, except a drip of blood seeped out from between his fingers. This time, she didn't give him the chance to protest. She moved quickly, jerking his wrists away from his face before he had time to react.

A deep gash from his forehead to his jaw sliced through his dark skin and over one eye. The blood seemed secondary as she took hold of his cheeks, pulling his face toward her. The eye. Had the sword sliced through his eye?

He pulled away and covered his face again. But she had seen what she needed. His eye suffered no damage.

Without another word, Talise scanned the desecrated gardens for a spare piece of cloth, preferably one that wasn't too dirty. A suitable cloth came from a nearby body. She refused to look at it as she tore a piece of fabric away from the cold skin.

Aaden wouldn't let her press the cloth against the blood. He stole it from her hands and turned his shoulder to her. He held his face at an angle so she couldn't see the injury. It didn't make any sense why he wouldn't let her help. Unless.

Was he embarrassed?

By this? He had fought against the Kessoku, even fought to protect her, and he was embarrassed about an injury from it?

But she didn't have time to consider that. In a heartbeat, she realized how quiet everything had gotten in the air around them. When she turned to look back at the palace, one lone Kessoku soldier stood staring at the palace.

The palace doors had been shut in her face and she stood all alone. She took one glance around the battlefield and the message was clear.

One survivor had been allowed. One survivor who could go back and tell Kessoku about the slaughter of the entire company. One survivor to make sure Kessoku never came back.

And then the woman was running. She jumped over bodies and clutched her sword. The veins in her face pulsed as she moved, desperate to get as far from the carnage as she could. When she disappeared over the ridge, Talise finally dared to move.

She pulled Aaden to his feet but let him keep his face hidden. As they tumbled back to the palace, his breath got heavier. Talise noticed the others also heading for the palace doors. Wendy, Claye, and the other palace guards.

When they got closer, the doors burst open, and Commander Blaise himself rushed out through them. He pushed his way through the tiny crowd and it suddenly hit her. He was heading for them.

Her gut twisted in horror. While gripping Aaden's elbow, Talise felt the muscles in his arm contract. She held onto him for dear life, fearing the commander's words.

He started speaking even before he reached them. "I expressly ordered that you two would not engage Kessoku after the mansion. What were you thinking?"

He had reached them now. Her knees knocked together as she swallowed. Commander Blaise reached for the cloth over Aaden's face, which Aaden gave up with no argument.

The commander's shoulders twitched at the sight of the blood. His face was a hardened slab of grit and determination. But that didn't stop a hint of horror shining through his eyes. He swallowed once and forced Aaden's cheek to the side so he could see it better.

"That will leave a scar." He spoke with precision, each word cutting through them both.

Aaden's eyes dropped further and further to the ground the longer the commander stared at him.

"I'm sorry, Grandfather," Aaden said in a tight voice.

Commander Blaise huffed, apparently unable to accept the apology.

"And *you*." The commander let out an exasperated sigh as he turned to Talise. He looked straight into her eyes, not allowing her to look away for even a moment. His exasperation turned to a hardened glare. He jabbed his pointer finger toward her chest. "You should have known better."

Talise's arms had frozen in place. A slice of terror cut through whatever resolve she had left. She blinked back at him, unable to think of a single retort.

He covered his eyes, shaking his head. Fear lined his words as he spoke. "What am I supposed to tell the emperor?"

She gulped again and gripped Aaden harder. It was only then that she remembered she was holding onto his arm. She swallowed and swallowed, trying to blink away her tears.

Commander Blaise spared her one more glance before he turned his back on them both.

"Go up to the library. I'll send a healer once the more serious injuries are dealt with."

Talise didn't let go of Aaden as they shuffled through the garden. Every time she swallowed all she could imagine was the emperor. What would he say about her decision to go back onto the battlefield? He might never forgive her.

# FIVE

**TALISE SNATCHED THE CLOTH FROM** Aaden's hand and threw it across the library before he could snatch it back. "You're being a baby," she said with exasperation. "Just let me look at it."

He folded his arms across his chest and turned away with an angry huff.

"Just." She wrapped her fingers around his chin and pushed his face toward her.

His skin warmed at her touch. She wondered if the heat had been on purpose or if he involuntarily warmed his veins just because she was around. Either way, she didn't have time to worry about it.

He didn't pull his chin out of her grip. For the briefest moment, he looked into her eyes. By the time she glanced back, he had looked away. And let out another huff.

She rolled her eyes at the reaction. "Would you calm down? One of the palace soldiers had his arm cut off. This is nothing."

He didn't respond. She had a feeling she had finally gotten to him, at least a little.

Now that she could examine the injury, it didn't look too bad. It was deep enough to scar, but it didn't go down to the bone. As long as the wound got cleaned, it shouldn't have any lasting damage.

"Hold still. I'm going to clean it."

Aaden's shoulders shifted. He tensed under her touch, but he seemed to finally accept the inevitable.

She shaped the water out of a nearby bowl. The bowl was still there from when she had brought it to the library early that morning. Back when a Kessoku scout group ravaged the palace and she thought it was nothing more than a trial.

She shook her head at her own naivety. With the water levitating in the air, Talise felt inside it for any trace of earth. A few minerals wouldn't be a problem, but to clean a wound, she needed clean water.

After concentrating for a few moments, she felt through the water and shaped the dirt and other contaminants out of it. For drinking, she would have left more of the minerals, but for cleaning, she removed them.

The wet patter of crumbs landed on the library table.

With the water clean, she shaped it over the slash in Aaden's face. It wasn't until the water rushed over his wound that she realized the water was getting in his eye. Maybe she should have found some salt to dissolve into the water so it wouldn't sting. But the salt would have made the wound dirty, so it was probably best she hadn't.

Her fingers moved in soft strokes through the air as she shaped the water in a steady flow over the wound. The dried blood at the edges of the wound came away freely. But deeper in the wound, it was harder to tell how clean it was.

Talise cupped her fingers under Aaden's chin and leaned closer to get a better angle. She'd propped herself atop one of the library tables so it would be easier to reach his face. Letting the water sink deeper into the wound, she leaned even closer still.

With her face close enough now, she could see how one of his eyes had more orange than the other. The left eye, the one with a gash running over it, had tiny spots of orange spiraling out from the pupils. The orange looked soft against the brown of his irises, almost like tiny chrysanthemums growing out of fresh summer soil.

She found her thumb stroking his cheek and immediately tipped his head up so he wouldn't recognize the motion for what it was.

When she was certain the wound was clean, she began shaping the water away from his face and into a ball above her palm. Two competing voices argued inside her head, one telling her to back away and run, the other telling her to move even closer.

Ignoring them both, she kept the water levitating while she visually inspected the wound. The healers would be able to do more than her, but the sooner the wound was clean, the better. She wondered how long it would take before it faded to a scar.

A heated finger traced over her bare shoulder, sending a shiver through her body. She had forgotten all about her own wound from the Kessoku soldier. And she hadn't realized it cut so much of her sleeve away.

"It doesn't hurt," Talise said as she dropped her hand away from Aaden's face. She shaped another ball of water out of a bowl. After removing the contaminants, she shaped the fresh water over her own wound, forcing Aaden to move his fingers off her skin.

The wound was nothing. Hardly a scratch when compared to the gash Aaden wore. Considering they had been attacked by a fairly angry soldier, it had been lucky to get away so clean.

She took extra time cleaning her wound because she had a feeling Aaden was itching to touch her skin again once the water was out of the way.

To prevent that from happening, Talise immediately hopped off the table as soon as she shaped the water away from her wound. Dropping the water back into the bowl, she carried the bowl to another table closer to the entrance of the library.

Whether he realized she was trying to get away from him or not, Aaden didn't move toward her. He fell into one of the library chairs and dropped his head in his hands. Dejected.

*But why*? Why should this injury mean so much to him?

After setting the bowl on the table, Talise was drawn back to the place she had been trying to avoid. When she sat down next to Aaden, he turned his face away from her so she couldn't see the wound.

"What is it?" she said, folding her arms over her chest. "Why are you so embarrassed?"

He scoffed in response. "Oh, of *course* I'm going to explain. Because you're so good about sharing things with me and all."

She flicked him in the arm which earned her a sharp gaze before Aaden remembered to turn his face away from her. "Are you afraid it's going to affect your shaping?" she asked.

"No."

"Are you worried the emperor won't like you with a scar?"

Aaden shifted one eyebrow upward as if the suggestion were a joke. It mostly was.

Talise tapped her chin with mock thoughtfulness. "Is it because you can see the wound out the corner of your eye, and you're worried it's going to distract you?"

"No." Aaden was shaking his head while wearing a frown.

But another thought entered her head. Her fingers were wrapped around his wrist before she even realized she'd moved them. "Did it affect your eyesight?"

This time his voice came out softer. "No." He stared at her fingers. "Stop asking me."

She pulled her hand away—maybe a little faster than necessary—and stuck it on her hip. "I won't stop asking until you tell me, so you might as well get it over with."

He let out a grunt that was probably supposed to sound a lot more irritated than it did. He hadn't quite removed the hint of pleasure in it. But then his shoulders dropped, and he looked away again. A heavy frown tugged the corners of his lips down. "It's stupid. Vanity. I know I shouldn't care, but..." He shook his head and buried his face once more.

When she pulled his hands away from his face, she did it gently. Not touching more than necessary, but not getting it over with quickly either. Once his hands weren't covering his eyes, she quirked an eyebrow up, begging him to tell more.

Finally, he let out a sigh of resignation. "My name, Aaden, comes from my great-grandfather. Apparently, he was known for being handsome. All the ladies pined after him. Most eligible bachelor in all the land, that sort of thing. When I was born, everyone said I was such a beautiful baby, so they named me after him."

He shook his head once more as he flexed his jaw. "I know it's stupid. I shouldn't care how handsome I am compared to the person I was named after. I just..." His shoulders slumped. "Now this scar will always remind me of how unfitting my name is."

He pressed his fingers into his elbow, staring at a knot in the wood of the table. His fingers kneaded over his elbow, back and forth while the muscles in his face seemed to droop.

Vanity? Maybe that would have been stupid, but this was different. He mourned something deeper than his words had said. Something a name represented. He mourned the connection he had to that great-grandfather. And now he felt like that connection was severed.

Or maybe he mourned his parents. It hadn't escaped her notice how he carefully omitted any mention of them when he told his little story. For the first time, she wondered what relationship he had with his father, if any.

"I'm sorry." It was all she could think to say. Almost as an afterthought, she said, "Names can have power. I understand feeling a loss because of one."

His eyes flicked to hers and the kneading over his elbow stopped. "Are you named after ...," his voice dropped, almost to a whisper, "Marmie?"

She shook her head, begging the tears to get back where they belonged. After a gulp, she said. "No, no one in my family is named Talise. It's just a name my parents liked. It's my middle name that has the loss."

It took her three heartbeats to work up the courage to say it. Three heartbeats full of terror. But she swallowed the fear, hoping she could smooth everything over without any suspicion. "Isla."

Aaden's eyebrows bounced upward as he leaned back in his chair. "The empress? You were named after her?"

Her nod was so tiny she worried he wouldn't see it. But of course he had.

She swallowed again and let her words out in a rush. "It was a popular name when I was born. Lots of children were named after her."

Aaden nodded in agreement. "Yeah, especially in the Crown. At least three different girls in my neighborhood were named Isla. Four if you include the princess."

Talise glanced at him, but she didn't dare speak. Afraid that any word would betray her.

He must have taken her silence for confusion. "The youngest princess," he said. "Her name was Isla too."

She nodded quickly. "Yes, I know that. I was just thinking, I'd forgotten you grew up so close to the palace. Did you ever meet the princess?"

He let out a long laugh and it surprised her how much she enjoyed seeing his smile. "No, I wasn't allowed to visit the palace when I was younger. I was too rowdy."

She let out a chuckle but found her eyes tracing the lines his smile made in his cheeks. When he glanced back at her, the warmth in his eyes seemed to penetrate her skin. She narrowed her eyes and leaned forward as if that was her plan all along.

"You don't need to worry anyway. It doesn't look bad." She made sure he could tell she was looking at the gash across his eye.

"Oh really?" he said wearing a smirk. "Are you calling me handsome?" He leaned forward, and her heart thundered in her chest.

Before either of them could react, the door to the library burst open. The emperor swept into the room, his silk tunic billowing behind him. His voice was gruff and low as he looked over his two Master Shapers. "Have the healers seen you yet?"

Talise was just lifting her head from a bow when she shifted to shake her head no.

The emperor looked them over again, his eyes lingering on Aaden's face a little longer than hers. He looked away only to stare at a wall. "I've been informed that a guard told you about the attack from Kessoku a few months ago."

The emperor lifted his head, not deigning to look down on them. "Now that you are aware, we will dismiss with the trials and have you train our newest recruits instead."

Talise blinked twice before the words sank in. The trials were over? Just like that? Apparently, they would both be staying.

The emperor nodded once, which wasn't strange. The strangest thing was the absence of certain words. Wasn't he going to criticize them for going back out among Kessoku after they had been told not to?

Perhaps he didn't know.

Since the emperor never missed an opportunity to criticize her, that must have been the only solution. But it gave Talise a bit of pause. Why would Commander Blaise withhold information from the emperor?

She shook the thought away. The emperor trusted the commander more than anyone. If the commander hadn't told him yet, maybe it was just because he hadn't had the time.

Emperor Flarius looked them over once more. "You will meet in the training hall tomorrow morning. I will be there to teach you how to train the soldiers."

Talise nodded, afraid to say anything that would turn his wrath toward her. Tomorrow she would begin leading the soldiers just like she was meant to do as Master Shaper. Finally, her years of training would allow her the position she'd been working for.

Now she could only wonder, would she succeed or fail?

# SIX

**THREE WEEKS HAD PASSED SINCE THE** latest attack on the palace. Talise and Aaden had finally taken their place as true Master Shapers, but it didn't feel like it at all. They'd been given the task of shape training the palace soldiers with yellow-hemmed tunics. These were the newest soldiers.

A handful of higher soldiers were also added to their classes. Those few with red, green, blue, or orange hems were soldiers who had achieved higher ranks based on their combat skills, but ones who still needed practice with the basics of combat shaping. Wendy worked with General Gale to teach advanced shape training to the higher ranked soldiers.

Each day, Talise and Aaden met the many groups of yellow-hemmed soldiers in the training hall, eager and willing to teach.

And each day, they were met with disappointment.

Talise fought to stay positive. She strived to only grumble when she was back in her living quarters. At the academy, she had been surrounded by such talented shapers she had forgotten most Kamdarians only received five years of shape training.

These new recruits seemed to struggle more than any of the students she had known. The ones with the red, green, blue, and orange hems were even worse. They were cocky since they were higher ranked, but their shaping skills were dismal. Things that were so simple to her, took great effort from them. Their sword, spear, and arrow skills were all impressive, but their shaping needed work.

A lot of it.

Talise stood at the head of the training hall wearing a blue training tunic and pants. The white belt tied around her waist had small silver swirls embroidered into it. That morning, she had thought dressing in blue might make her seem more relatable. It might help the soldiers see her as a shaper whose primary was water, rather than a Master Shaper and the only shaper in history to conquer ice shaping.

The idea had been ridiculous. She realized it only a few minutes into the morning. The soldiers stumbled over their training the same as they always did. Even simple things like throwing a fire ball took more effort than it should have.

"Like this," Talise said, straining to force a smile. Her left foot was positioned slightly behind her right. The stance was the same as dagger throwing, so it shouldn't have been hard. Even the yellow-hemmed soldiers were decent at dagger throwing.

She held her palm flat in front of her chest, shaping a fire ball in front of it. When she pushed her hand forward, the fire ball soared until it landed squarely in the center of the bull's eye where she aimed.

She turned back to the soldiers with what she hoped was an encouraging smile. "Go on," she said, hopefully not as strained as she felt. "Try again."

The squad of soldiers turned to face their targets and did the move just as she had done. Except none of them did it like her at all. One soldier stood with her feet right next to each other. She lost her balance when she punched the fire ball forward.

One soldier pushed his palm forward slowly, as if pushing a curtain aside. His fire ball lazily fell to the ground only a few steps in front of him. He sucked in a breath as he quickly stomped on it to put the fire out.

The other soldiers did no better. The one closest to her hadn't even produced a flame. He scratched his head as he turned to Talise. "Where does fire shaping come from again? The veins?"

"The heart," she replied with a sigh. "Not the veins, the heart."

She held in a second sigh and glanced over at Aaden. He was shaking his head at the soldiers looking as frustrated as she felt. They'd been working with different squads all morning. She was certain this one had been the worst.

Making a quick decision, she snapped her fingers at the soldiers. They dropped their hands to their sides and stood at attention. She decided to ignore how much slower they moved than they usually did for the emperor or Commander Blaise.

"We're going to finish a little early today. Go on down to the kitchens and see if dinner is ready."

She expected them to be excited. Maybe be grateful for her generosity. Instead, they nodded with hardly any expression and left the room. She wanted to whack them upside the head and force gratitude from their lips. Though, she suspected that wouldn't be an effective way to earn their trust.

Aaden was still shaking his head as he walked down the room to look at the targets. "Pathetic," he muttered under his breath. "Fire balls should be easy."

Talise let out an exasperated sigh as she grabbed the nearest target to put it away. "I didn't think it would be this hard. Shouldn't palace soldiers be capable of basic shaping before they get recruited?"

Aaden shrugged. "They accept anyone into the palace army. That's the big pull, you know. They'll take anyone who's willing and then feed them and give them a place to live. A lot of the soldiers are probably only here because they couldn't find a job anywhere else."

The muscles in her arms shivered as she grabbed the next target. She thought it best not to mention that not *everyone* was accepted into the palace army. Not people from the Storm. And those people needed the food and shelter more than anyone.

She rubbed a thumb over the hem of her tunic, staring absently into the training hall. "I thought we would have more help. I thought the other Master Shapers would be here. I thought we'd have more resources to help us. Instead, it feels like we've been given nothing, and we're expected to turn the army into shaping prodigies."

"Maybe you're putting too much pressure on yourself," Aaden said, grabbing the last target. "No one ever said we have to get them shaping at a certain level."

Talise gritted her teeth. "The emperor implied it. You know he did. He expects us to have them shooting perfect fire balls by Fire Festival. Which is utterly ridiculous. He expects too much and then refuses to give us the resources we need to deliver."

"It is unwise to speak ill of your emperor at any time."

Talise froze as Emperor Flarius's voice filled the training hall.

"But especially when you are in a large room where anyone can hear."

Talise gulped before she turned around to bow deeply to her sovereign. Aaden's head dropped almost as low as hers.

The emperor sneered at them both. She raised her head slowly, afraid of the punishment awaiting her.

"You blame others, when the fault is your own."

His words weren't so terrible, but like always, they cut her to her core. The emperor had a way of finding the truths she tried to ignore.

"We are so sorry, Your Imperial Highness." Aaden bowed again, his words more submissive than usual.

More than anything else, Aaden's reaction was the biggest indicator that they were really in trouble this time. She should have known better than to speak against in the emperor in such an open room. Her mounting frustration was no excuse.

The emperor ignored Aaden completely as he stepped toward Talise. "You have shaping skills, but you know nothing about being a leader."

She gulped and took a step back, unconsciously trying to put as much distance between herself and the emperor as possible.

"You complain about the soldier's lack of progress, but you are the real problem. *You* are the only reason these lessons are failing."

Her bottom lip trembled as she fought to regain control of her emotions. She kept her head high. "I'm doing the best I can."

The emperor scoffed in response. "Then maybe you aren't worthy of the authority you think you deserve. A true leader doesn't complain about the incompetence of soldiers. A true leader looks within to solve problems."

His words only hurt because they were true. She pinched the bridge of her nose as she looked away. "I'm trying, but nobody taught me how to teach. I only know how to shape. I don't understand what I'm doing wrong."

"You have none of the natural leadership you need. None of it!"

Those words hurt more than they should have. All she could think about were the people she knew who *did* have natural leadership skills. Marmie was the top of the list. Marmie always found ways to inspire confidence, but she never used cruel words like the emperor did.

The emperor was highly respected too. There was an element of fear there, but it wasn't just that. He took care of Kamdaria, and the people knew it.

The emperor frowned. He stood a step toward her, towering above. "You must do better than this. Their lack of progress isn't acceptable. Do you understand?"

A wave of tears stung in her eyes. She wanted to scream and sob all at once.

Aaden came closer. "Do you have any tips?" His voice was submissive again, but now that Talise knew it so well, she could hear the edge in it.

The emperor ignored him and stepped even closer. He pinched her chin between his thumb and forefinger, forcing her face up to meet his eyes. "Do you understand?" he asked again.

Her bottom lip trembled no matter how hard she clenched her jaw. She tried to stop the tears, but they fell before she could do anything about it. Her heart ached inside. All she wanted was to be back in the Storm. She wanted to sit on the dirt floor of the crumbling mud hut and huddle in front of the tiny fire. Their bellies had been empty, but there wasn't as much pressure.

There wasn't as much pain.

Talise tried to take in a breath, but it came in a staccato, shuddering with her silent sobs. "I'm trying," she said through a sniff.

Emperor Flarius had no sympathy for her tears. His face was unflinching. Demanding. He wouldn't accept anything less than perfection. "Try harder."

She tried to pull her chin away, tried to escape his grasp, but he pinched tighter still. His eyes bore into her, making her feel not just like an incompetent child, but like a burden. A mistake.

Her lip trembled while a fresh set of tears left her eyes. She kept trying to stop, but each attempt was only met with more tears.

The emperor opened his mouth to speak again, but Aaden stepped near enough to catch his eye. He held his arms at his sides, both hands in tight fists, one gripping a short training rod. Through clenched teeth he said, "Stop it."

The emperor eyed Aaden carefully. His face showed no intention of stopping, but he did let his hand fall away from Talise's chin. The moment the emperor's hand left her face, Aaden took a step closer, forcing his shoulder between her and the emperor.

Raising an eyebrow, the emperor said, "It isn't your place to question my methods." He turned to Talise again, having to crane his neck to see past Aaden. "I expect—"

"I said, *stop it*." Aaden took another step to the side, fully blocking Talise from the emperor's view. He used one hand to push her back behind him. While she feared how his actions would get him in trouble, she couldn't bring herself to stop him. She needed a break from the emperor's eyes. If only for a moment.

Stuck behind Aaden, she couldn't see the emperor's face, but it was easy to imagine the haughty expression that went along with his words. "You do *not* tell me what to do. I am the emperor."

"I don't care," Aaden said, his voice even and unforgiving.

Talise managed to silence the gasp that tried to escape. It didn't matter now if she wanted a break from the emperor. If Aaden continued like this, he would be thrown into the dungeon, she was sure of it.

She grasped his arm and forced him to face her. "Don't do this," she said in a whisper. "Just leave. I can handle it."

He gave her a careful look. One of his hands still gripped the short training rod, but the other relaxed. She knew he was about to reach for her.

"I will train my Master Shapers in any way I see fit." The emperor's voice rang through the training room. Loud and not allowing any argument in return.

Aaden whipped around, the muscles in his neck tensing. "You leave her alone."

She tightened her grip on his arm. "Stop, Aaden. I don't need you to do this."

He looked into her eyes then. She understood the dilemma going on in his head. She knew he didn't understand why she refused his protection. But it didn't matter if he understood. She just needed him to listen.

She stared back, pleading with her eyes. Not explaining but begging him to let it go. The longer he stared, the more he seemed to understand. She wouldn't let him do this for her. And for some reason, he seemed hurt by that.

The emperor balled his hands into fists and held them in front of his chest. The movement brought both her and Aaden's attention to him. Probably just as he intended. He gave a measured glance to Aaden. Even without words, the look spoke volumes.

It was a threat. Not just a threat, but a promise. Finally, the emperor said, "If you try to stop me again, I will strip away your title of Master Shaper and send you to the Storm where you belong."

This at least gave Aaden pause. He sucked in a shallow breath, but his fear was soon outweighed. By what, Talise didn't know, but it felt like something noble. He glanced back at her, and she could see it in his eyes. He was willing to fight for her, no matter the cost.

Drawing her eyebrows together, she gave her head the tiniest shake, willing him to stop fighting. Again, she begged using nothing more than her expression.

He stared back, begging in his own way. Showing her that he wanted to help.

But she wouldn't let him.

His face fell, and he let out a huff. "Fine." He threw the training rod to the ground with a clatter. He gave one last glance to Talise and the emperor before turning his back on both of them. "But I'm not going to stand here and watch."

As he marched out of the room, she waited for the emperor to condemn him. To punish him for leaving without being dismissed. But he never did. The emperor merely stared at the back of

Aaden's head before it disappeared through the doorway.

As usual, his face was a blank slate, impossible to read. He turned back to her. The muscles in his face stayed frozen in place as he spoke. "Fire Festival is coming. There will be a masquerade ball here at the palace the evening of Fire Festival. If you haven't proven your ability to lead before then, I'll send you back to the Storm."

Her nose wrinkled at his words. Every vein inside her was on fire, burning through her fear. "You wouldn't," she said, daring to let a hint of the anger escape.

He shrugged. "A Master Shaper must be able to lead." With a small glance in her eyes, he said, "Intimidation is effective, but it's not the only method."

With that, he turned on his heel and marched away. Gritting her teeth together, she slammed her fist into her palm. When that did nothing to improve her mood, she shaped a fire ball only to slam it against the wall. After the fire ball, she sent a wave of air to crash into a nearby shelf.

The wind hit the shelf with a great shudder, sending several bowls through the air only to shatter into pieces when they hit the ground. She let out a scream.

No matter what, she would not use intimidation. It didn't matter how effective it was, she had no desire to be anything like the emperor.

And now she had to prepare for Fire Festival. She had been so wrapped up in the competition and then the trials, she hadn't realized how close the mid-summer holiday was.

The weeks leading up to Fire Festival usually involved all sorts of ancient traditions that were supposed to be fun. Now, she guessed those weeks would only be stressful.

She let out a breath, trying to calm her racing heart. At least with the masquerade ball, she'd have one good thing. Now she had a chance to use one of the many gowns tucked in the wardrobe in her living quarters.

# SEVEN

**TALISE SHOVED ANOTHER GOWN BACK** into her wardrobe. The silky red orange dress was beyond beautiful. A huge ball gown skirt with a thick bodice that would hide any imperfections in the stomach area. The long sleeves made the dress look more regal than anything. The smooth velvet fabric was perfect.

As gorgeous as it was, the long sleeves and velvet were impractical for Fire Festival. She needed something that would allow her to breathe on a hot summer evening.

She ran her fingers over an ivory gown with delicate blue flowers, but she wouldn't allow herself to look at it closely. It didn't matter how beautiful it was, she couldn't wear a blue gown to Fire Festival.

Just then, a timid knock came at the door to her living quarters. After shutting the wardrobe, she skipped through her bedroom and into the sitting room. When she opened the door, a wave of disappointment washed over her at the sight of Wendy. But she wasn't sure why. She hadn't been expecting anyone else, so why should she care that Wendy was there?

Wendy chewed on her bottom lip as she kept her head tilted down. Looking up through her eyelashes she said, "Can I come in?"

The guilt inside Talise came on strong, but she did nothing to temper the feeling. It had been three weeks since Kessoku's attack, and Talise had only seen Wendy once since then. That conversation hadn't lasted long.

Wendy's throat contracted as she swallowed.

Talise pressed her lips into a thin line. "I'm a busy with—"

"I know you're avoiding me." Her voice was soft and sweet, but a real pain danced through it.

Talise's stomach clenched in a knot. Now she was the one who swallowed. "No, I've just been busy. I haven't had time for..." Her voice trailed off. It didn't matter what excuses she had been feeding herself over the last three weeks. She *was* mad at Wendy. But she also missed her. Ever since coming to the palace, they had seen each other less and less. And Talise needed her best friend back.

All at once, Wendy's eyes filled with tears. She must have been working hard to hold them back because they slid down her cheeks in steady streams. "I'm sorry I didn't tell you about Kessoku. I know you hate me for it. I didn't know very much. And General Gale said the emperor would execute me if I said anything." When a hiccup escaped her mouth, she clasped her hands over it and closed her eyes.

All the anger Talise had been harboring shattered with wave of sympathy. "Oh, stop that," she said, pulling Wendy into the room.

Once the door was closed, Talise let out a sigh. "I know they threatened to hurt you if you said anything. And I know I shouldn't have been mad."

Wendy gave a knowing frown. "I would have been mad too. I thought of all the people they would tell it would be the Master Shapers."

Talise nodded, grateful someone else shared her exasperation.

With a sniff, Wendy carefully tucked a piece of her long, black hair behind her ear. "But I guess since the other Master Shapers were killed, maybe they didn't want you to worry you'd be next."

This didn't seem likely to Talise. They probably just didn't want the rest of Kamdaria finding out how close Kessoku got *again* to murdering the emperor. But she wasn't about to dwell on that. She'd already spent enough energy being angry over the last few weeks.

Talise found a handkerchief inside her desk and handed it to Wendy. "How much did you know?" she asked.

Wendy blew her nose for a long time before answering. The resulting sound seemed louder than a crashing avalanche. Far too loud to have come from her timid friend. When she finished blowing, Wendy whimpered and dabbed at the corners of her eyes. In a flash, it seemed impossible the horrendous noise had ever occurred. That thought made Talise want to snicker.

Clutching the handkerchief close to heart, Wendy dropped her lips into a frown. "It all started with the letter from my brother. It didn't sound like it came from him. I kept asking questions and one of the soldiers finally admitted it didn't come from Cyrus at all."

"Then who wrote it?"

"One of the palace soldiers," Wendy said through her teeth. "After I found out, I went straight to General Gale and demanded answers.

He didn't tell me everything. He just said Cyrus might still be alive, but they didn't know for sure. And he also told me Kessoku was more dangerous than everyone thought. That's it. That's all I knew. I had no idea they were going to attack the palace."

Talise began pacing the floor. "Why didn't they tell you Cyrus was missing? If they didn't tell you or your parents, that means none of the other families know either. How can they justify keeping secrets like that?"

But Wendy wasn't listening to her. She had found the door to Talise's bedroom and her mouth hung open, her eyes transfixed on something inside the room. "Your rooms are so much bigger than mine. And they're so fancy."

A cold thread of guilt tripped over the knot in Talise's stomach. She managed a little shrug. "I think it's because I'm a Master Shaper."

"I should have trained harder," Wendy said tracing the carving that adorned Talise's doorframe. "I had no idea Master Shapers had it so good."

This brought a chuckle to Talise's lips. And it gave her an idea. "Do you have a gown for Fire Festival? There's going to be a masquerade ball."

Wendy's eyes lit up. "A ball?" But then she twirled a bit of her hair over a finger. "I've made a little money since working here, but I don't know if—"

Talise cut her off by grabbing her wrist and yanking her into the bedroom. She threw open the wardrobe and let the gowns burst out.

A twinkle appeared in Wendy's eyes as she reached for the delicate fabrics.

"Do you think one of these will work?" Talise asked. "You can borrow one."

Wendy laughed as she pulled out a burgundy gown with gold beads decorating the bodice. The color was dark, but the chiffon fabric was light and airy, making it perfect for a summer evening.

Wendy's mouth seemed to have stopped working. Her jaw dropped further as she held the dress up to her body. The gold beads had been sewed into intricate patterns and lines. In the center of the bodice, swirls of gold beads funneled down to the waistline, creating an abstract tornado shape. Perfect for a shaper whose primary was air.

Talise pulled her friend across the room so she could admire the dress in front of the mirror. When Wendy saw herself with the dress, she twirled around as if unable to stop herself.

"Try it on," Talise said, grinning. "See how it fits."

Soon they were both in gowns. They giggled over paper fans as they pretended to flirt with invisible suitors. When they tired of that, Talise dragged Wendy into the bathroom and forced her to use the cosmetics.

Wendy didn't wear cosmetics regularly, but she certainly had more experience than Talise. After an embarrassing amount of time, Talise finally produced a perfect line of black paint above her eyelashes. It ended in a sharp point at the corner of her eye.

When she attempted a similar line over the other eye, it resulted in a sloppy mess and Talise gave up with a snort.

"Are you going to wear this one, then?" Wendy asked, touching the black sleeve of Talise's jewel encrusted gown.

Talise shrugged in response. "I guess. I liked the tangerine one too, but it's a little bright for my taste."

Wendy tapped her chin thoughtfully before she ran into the bedroom to dig into the wardrobe. "Oh Talise," she said, emitting a soft gasp. "What about this one? It's perfect."

The ivory dress came out of the wardrobe and the light glinted off the shiny blue embroidery thread. No matter how Talise had tried to ignore it earlier, she couldn't help gazing at it now.

The ivory silk started at the top with delicate cap sleeves and ended with a thick ball gown bottom. A layer of white tulle covered the ivory silk. In the tulle, blue flowers had been embroidered. The flowers were thick around the waist of the dress then became sparse around the hem and neckline.

Breathtaking.

If only the emperor weren't so obsessed with fire shaping. She let out a sigh that carried all the way from the bathroom door where she stood to the wardrobe where Wendy held the dress. "I can't wear blue to Fire Festival. The emperor would never forgive me for broadcasting myself as having a preference for water shaping. The flowers are gorgeous though."

"Flowers?" Wendy asked, tilting her head to the side. "No, look at them carefully. They aren't flowers at all."

With curiosity moving her, Talise stepped across the room. After only a few steps, she realized why Wendy was so excited. They *weren't* flowers. Instead, small blue flames burst out around tiny dots. They looked like flowers from a distance, but up close, the flame shape was obvious. The dress was covered in blue *fire*.

Talise's mouth dropped in awe. She didn't protest when Wendy held the dress up to her shoulders and forced her in front of the mirror.

With a honey sweet smile, Wendy clapped her hands together. "It's like this dress was made for you. Everyone knows you're the first ice shaper in Kamdaria, so it's fitting for you to wear blue. But the flames..." her voice lingered off while they both admired the exquisite embroidery.

Not even the emperor himself could find fault with this dress. Orange was traditionally the color associated with fire, but blue flames did exist. Wendy was right. The dress was perfect.

Staring at the ivory silk made it easy to ignore her deeper problems. But the more she tried to ignore them, the more quickly they came to the forefront of her mind. Talise started to put the dress away, unable to focus on it anymore.

Noticing the change in her demeanor, Wendy asked, "What's wrong?"

Talise bit her bottom lip, trying to decide how much to share. Finally, she said, "I'm trying to teach the soldiers fire shaping, but apparently they don't even know basic combat shaping. I don't know what to do."

Wendy scratched her ear and looked away. She didn't say anything for a while. When she did, she finally said, "I know a few books in the library that might help."

It was easy to let the smile shine through her face. She'd spent three weeks being angry at Wendy for lying to her. And all this time she could have had help with her greatest trouble if only she'd asked.

"Let me change out of this dress and I'll show you," Wendy said.

Talise nodded and let hope blossom through her. With Wendy's help, maybe she had a chance of figuring this out.

# EIGHT

**CONVERSATION CAME EASILY AS** Talise and Wendy entered the library. Wendy had told her the titles of a few books, but they hadn't found them yet. When they turned the corner to check another shelf, Talise almost ran into a pair of young men.

Her interest piqued when she saw Aaden standing not alone, but with Claye. Her neck flushed with heat when she saw Aaden, just like it always did, but the heat vanished almost as quickly. Her stomach dropped.

Aaden tried to hide his face, but he seemed to realize it was already too late. He was right about that.

Talise gripped her stomach, unable to form words. Instead, Wendy formed them for her. "What happened to your face?"

Aaden's jaw flexed, which made the purple bruise on his chin bulge. He had another, darker bruise gracing the eye that had a gash running over it.

Two bruises. Both fresh.

A sinking feeling at the pit of her stomach told Talise who had given them to him. Her mind immediately went back to the last time she'd seen Aaden. He had disrespected the emperor and then stormed off without being dismissed.

He had been trying to protect her, which made him seem more honorable in her eyes. The emperor clearly had seen it the opposite way.

A wave of nausea churned in her stomach, forcing her to clutch it again. She wanted to hear what happened. But Aaden only stared at Wendy, unable to answer her question, and suddenly Talise understood. He didn't want anyone else to know what had happened. She could understand that. If everyone knew the emperor had hit him, or made one of his guards do it, they would think less of Aaden.

When Aaden remained silent, Claye chimed in. He shrugged and said, "Yeah, he won't tell me either. Are you wearing eyeliner?" He finished by taking one step too close into Talise's personal space.

Heat burned through her cheeks as she remembered the perfect line over her right eye accompanied by the sloppy line over her right. "Oh yeah," she said attempting a chuckle. "We were practicing for the ball."

Claye quirked one eyebrow up. "I thought it was a masquerade ball. No one would be able to see your eyes anyway."

Unable to respond, Talise merely blinked back at him. Why hadn't *she* thought of that?

Wendy glanced at Aaden once more, but apparently gave up on learning more about his bruises. Instead, she leaned over Claye's arm to look at the book in his hand.

"Why are you reading about the emperor's genealogy?" she asked.

"That is an excellent question," Claye said with a smile. "Come see what we're working on."

Wendy followed Claye, which gave Talise a brief moment to be alone with Aaden. Unfortunately, he seemed unwilling to let her use it. Instead, he gestured toward Claye and Wendy. "You should see this too."

When they made it to the table where Claye and Aaden had been earlier, Wendy peered over the books. "You said one of the Kessoku soldiers stole the emperor's family tree from the treasury?"

Claye nodded. "Yes, and we're trying to figure out why. The public records only mention the emperor's five youngest children by first name. That's standard until they become adults. But some of the empress's family isn't well known either. There must be additional information on the family tree that isn't in the public records."

Talise sat down in the chair next to Claye, trying not to notice how Aaden scooted his chair closer to hers.

Claye lowered his voice to a whisper, careful to let his words have the highest possible impact. "We think Kessoku is looking for an heir. If they can't kill the emperor, at least they can make sure he has no one to pass the throne to, right?"

When Wendy let out a faint gasp, Claye smirked with satisfaction. He glanced at Talise to see her reaction.

She raised one eyebrow, careful to let him see her skepticism. "Is there any evidence of an heir?"

Claye opened his mouth excitedly, but a moment later his face fell. "No. Sadly, there is not. But..." He raised one finger, that excitement crawling back again. "Look what we found."

He pointed to one of the open books on the table. "These are accounts from people who attended the funeral after the royal family was murdered. Look at this one."

*The empress looked as beautiful as ever lying in her grave box. The little children from the Crown left chrysanthemums beside her, knowing it was her favorite flower. The empress's sister suffered a far worse fate. Her face was mangled beyond recognition. I could hardly look at it for fear of being sick.*

The details brought the funeral to life in Talise's eye. It took great effort to see past them and try to discover what had made Claye so excited. When she couldn't figure it out, she looked up at him with another skeptical frown.

"What's so interesting about this?"

Claye jabbed the paragraph with his finger. "The empress's sister! Mangled beyond recognition? Doesn't that seem suspicious to you?"

Talise shrugged, unwilling to play along with his excitement. The emperor had seven children, two daughters-in-law, and a grandson who had all been killed in the attack. The empress, the empress's sister, and their parents were also killed. None of it seemed like information that needed to be resurfaced.

Wendy's face screwed up into a knot. "Didn't Kessoku use boulders in their attack? I thought a lot of the victims were mangled beyond recognition."

Claye let out a huff before falling back into his seat. "She was the only member of the family who was mangled like that. It does seem suspicious."

Talise leaned closer to look, scanning the rest of the account before flipping through a few more pages. Absently, she said, "What would Kessoku want with the emperor's sister-in-law anyway? The empress was only royal by marriage. Her sister wouldn't be an heir even if she were alive."

"That's what *I* said," Aaden said in a low voice.

Claye threw his hands into the air. "Well, I don't know. Maybe Kessoku doesn't want an heir. Maybe they're trying to get the empress's sister on their side. That could be a powerful symbol, you know. If they turned someone who was so close to the emperor."

"But why look now?" Talise asked. "It's been twelve years since the attack."

He jutted out his bottom lip by way of response.

Always quick to dispel contention, Wendy reached for his hand and gave a sweet smile. "Aren't you excited about the masquerade ball for Fire Festival? You could dance with that pretty soldier you're always talking about."

Claye showed a hint of smile after that, his anger subsiding for a moment. He rolled his shoulders back with an air of confidence. "I *have* wooed many women with my dancing skills. She'd probably fall for me if I got her to dance."

"But I thought..." Aaden's voice stopped abruptly as he glanced from Claye to Wendy and then back again. When they only stared back in response, he pointed between them. "I thought you two were..." He blinked, willing one of them to finish his sentence. When no one did, he finally said, "You know, in love or something."

Talise couldn't help her eyebrows from flying up to her forehead. Wendy let out a snort, which Claye pretended to be offended by. A moment later, he was laughing. He wrapped his arms around both Talise and Wendy and pulled them in close. "Sadly. These two know way too many embarrassing things about me to ever see me romantically."

Aaden blinked again. Not so subtly, his eyes drifted away from Claye's face and over to the arm that was now wrapped tight around Talise's shoulder. "Oh," he said, a bit anticlimactically.

"I just had an idea," Talise said, jumping out of her chair. "Do you remember how Mrs. Dew made us hold those hot rocks close to our heart? It was back when you two first came to the elite academy. She made us hold them so we could feel the heat in our hearts. It helped us shape fire better because we could feel that it came from the heart. I think it might work for the soldiers too."

Aaden followed after her when she left the library. She was grateful the other two didn't. He must have forgotten about the bruises on his face, but she hadn't. Once they were alone, she would get him to talk.

# NINE

**TALISE WAITED UNTIL THEY WERE FAR** down the hall before she attempted conversation. She even glanced over her shoulder to make sure there were no prying ears she hadn't noticed.

Aaden seemed mildly interested when she looked over her shoulder, but then he seemed to realize her true intention all at once. His jaw flexed and he began to walk faster.

When she touched his arm, his steps faltered. "What happened?"

He wouldn't look at her. He shifted his arm out of her grip and turned his head the other way. "Does it matter what size the rocks are? Can they be pebbles from the garden or do we need to find bigger ones?"

"Aaden." She stepped in front of him, forcing him to a stop. She held her bottom lip between her teeth for a moment, desperate to keep it from trembling. "What did he do to you?"

That was her only real question. She already knew exactly what happened and why. But were there more injuries she couldn't see? How bad were they?

He shifted away again, making eye contact impossible. But then his shoulder twitched as he looked back for one small moment.

"You have to tell me." Her voice was higher than she meant it to be.

He folded his arms over his chest, turning away again. Every sign made it clear he would not discuss the incident. Desperation took over. She did the only thing she could think of.

She reached for his arm. Letting her fingers slide over his warm skin, she let them land over his hand. And finally, she wrapped her fingers over his, squeezing just enough that he couldn't ignore it.

His gaze fell to her hand much quicker than she expected. He abandoned all hope of ignoring her and turned to face her instead. Using his thumb, he held her fingers into place over his hand. When he looked at her, a sadness lingered in his eyes that she had never seen before. "Why do you let him talk to you like that?"

Her shoulders dropped. Her heartbeat slowed to a thundering pulse. "*Let* him? I can't control what he says to me."

Aaden looked away. He unfolded his arms just enough to pull her fingers closer to his chest. Each of his breaths sounded heavier than the last. "Yes, but you worry so much about his words."

A weight seemed to drop on her chest, making it difficult to breathe. She chewed her bottom lip, afraid to speak. The truth was too painful to speak, but it was also too painful to ignore. "Everything he says is true."

Aaden looked up, exasperation in his eyes. "Yes, that. *That* is exactly what I'm talking about. You take his words too hard. Why do you care so much? Why is his approval so important to you?"

"He's the emperor." Her words came out with a sense of finality. It should have been impossible to argue with her logic.

He didn't even try. His arms unfolded from in front of his chest, but he managed to keep a tender grip on her hand. He looked deeper into her eyes which sent a trill through the furthest edges of her body. Without a word, his argument was clear.

Some people's opinions were more important than others.

Still communicating in silence, he was making a pretty strong argument for his opinion being the only one she should care about. She had a feeling his argument would include some more nonverbal communication soon. Particularly one that involved lips.

Most of her wanted to give in without any thought to the consequences. Yet, another part of her worried what his attitude meant. If he didn't think the emperor's opinion was important, what did that say about his honor? Was he only being loyal to the emperor because it kept him out of the Storm?

If he didn't actually respect the emperor's authority, then how was he any different from Kessoku? He wasn't actively trying to murder the emperor. That did make him significantly different from Kessoku, right? But was the difference significant enough?

Another moment of looking into his eyes and she wouldn't have cared anymore. But before he could lean in, the jovial laughter of nearby soldiers interrupted the silence. The soldiers were just around the corner and soon their words became crystal clear.

"It's their own fault for expecting us to make fire balls after a few weeks of training," said a female voice. "The other Master Shapers always started their training with air."

Talise gave a nervous glance to Aaden while she backed up closer to the wall. It didn't warm her heart to know the soldiers were talking about them behind their backs, but it probably would have been even less pleasant for the soldiers to run into the pair of them while they were doing it.

Following her lead, Aaden pushed open the door to the training hall. They both slipped inside moments before the soldiers appeared around the corner.

"Who do they think they are anyway?" A gruff voice said, in contrast to the earlier one. "She's just a girl from the Storm and he's the son of a traitor. They come in here thinking they're better than us because they're Master Shapers, but they're both nothing more than vermin."

"You said it," agreed the female soldier.

Talise held her breath as the soldiers passed by the training hall door. Her heart raced as their steps echoed down the hallway.

The soldiers didn't trust her. They looked down on her. She had to accept that now.

All this time she thought the title of Master Shaper was all she needed to lead. In one short conversation, these soldiers had proved her wrong.

The emperor's words from the day before rang in her ears. *A true leader doesn't complain about the incompetence of soldiers. A true leader looks within to solve problems.*

If she kept complaining about her soldiers' inability to shape, she'd never get anywhere.

When they were far past the training hall door, she turned to Aaden with a start. Pointing toward the hallway, she said, "That is why I care about the emperor's words. Like I said before, everything he says is true."

# TEN

**THE LIBRARY WAS ALWAYS A VAST** source of knowledge, but for the first time in her life, Talise wasn't sure what to look for. The polished wood shelves towered high above her. Rolling ladders were attached to the end of each long row so the highest shelves would be reachable.

She loved the musty smell of the old books. Sometimes she would lean in close just to breathe in the smell. And the spines were always so lovely. Leather and cloth with such designs on the cover, as beautiful and intricate as pieces of art.

She traced a finger over a friendly green spine. The title had seemed silly at first, but she kept coming back to it. Glancing over her shoulder, she checked to see if Aaden was nearby. He wasn't.

They were supposed to be looking for books that would help them be better teachers. She had already spent the last two days poring over books on teaching theory. The strategies were helpful, but they tended to focus on concrete concepts like management and curriculum design.

What she needed was much more abstract. Loyalty, respect. Not for the first time that day, her thoughts drifted back to Marmie. Even in her earliest memories, Talise recognized how Marmie could gain the respect of anyone around her.

Marmie had been firm when she needed to be, but she had never treated Talise the way the emperor did. What was it about Marmie that made her so endearing to everyone she met?

Talise traced her finger over the title again. *Eternal Friendships*. A part of her still felt silly about it. What did friendship have to do with leadership? But another part of her felt like it might be the answer she needed.

When she attempted to abandon the competition back at the academy, Wendy had packed food for her. She implored her to stay, but she never forced her to.

It wasn't a title or intimidation that made Wendy react the way she did. In that case, friendship was all she needed.

Glancing over her shoulder for a second time, Talise pulled the book off the shelf. Enough of the going back and forth. She needed answers, and she needed them now. Fire Festival was only two weeks away. She didn't have time to waste.

The first few pages held words that should have seemed obvious.

*More than anything, a friendship blossoms when both parties are genuinely invested in the other's lives. If an eternal friendship is what you desire, begin by asking about the person's life. But that is only the first step. Next, it is imperative that both parties then support each other and help each other succeed in their desired goals.*

She wanted to roll her eyes at the words. She wanted to scoff and laugh and write the book off as useless. Except she couldn't. As obvious as the words were, she couldn't help but realize she had never once made any attempt to get to know her soldiers.

Their hopes and desires were mysteries to her. She knew nothing of their families, their homes. When she passed by them in the halls, they were like moving statues. Nothing more than decorations or tools.

A knot twisted through her stomach as she continued to read. How had she lived seventeen years and never realized how incredibly self-involved she was? She knew the servants and soldiers had their own lives and troubles. So, why had she never thought to care about them?

This was a problem. A problem that bit into her. She had been so self-absorbed, so desperate to win the competition, that she'd barely been able to see outside of her own life.

Her stomach wrenched. If she'd grown up the rest of her life in the Storm, this wouldn't have happened. Marmie would have taught her to be kind to people, to be invested in their lives.

She gritted her teeth and rolled her shoulders back. *No.* Hating herself for past mistakes would fix nothing. She had done wrong to ignore her soldiers and expect their respect when she'd done nothing to earn it. But she didn't have to continue doing wrong.

Balancing the open book on her hands, she read as she walked back to the table. She scanned the words with voracious interest, trying to soak them all in. She found herself reading certain passages several times, trying to commit them to memory. At one point, she nearly underlined a particular passage for its utter truth.

*True friendship is about building each other up, not using the other for gain.*

She wanted to pull out her hair for being so stupid. This whole time she saw the soldiers as nothing more than tools, weapons. Of course they hated her. They had every right to.

She had already gotten a quarter of the way through the book before Aaden joined her at the table. He carried another theory of teaching book, but his fingers pinched the book at the corner, as if the book wasn't worth the effort of holding it properly.

"Looks like you were more successful than me. Should I read that one too?"

She bit her bottom lip, ignoring his question altogether. Instead, she asked one of her own. "Have you talked with any of the soldiers? More than to give them orders, I mean. Do you know any of their names? Any of their dreams?"

The very thought made Aaden chuckle. "I'm not very good with people. I'm sure you've noticed."

"Sit down by me," she said, and as always, he looked more than happy to comply. "We need to read this together.

"I WISH THERE weren't so many of them all together."

Talise eyed the group of four soldiers from around the corner. "I know," she said, lengthening out the syllables so her exasperation was clear. She tucked the green book under her elbow as she swallowed.

"Come on, we've already read the whole book twice. We have to do this now."

Aaden nodded, setting his face with determination. Even as he struggled to focus, the terror in his eyes was clear.

She might have laughed at him if her own expression hadn't been an exact mirror of his. They both took a deep breath before they waltzed around the corner toward the soldiers.

The soldiers grimaced at the sight of them. Two of the soldiers turned their backs on them. Had she been such a terrible leader that even looking at her was such a task now?

She shoved the thought away, not giving it residence in her mind. The past was behind her. All she could do was move forward the right way.

"Hello." Aaden's greeting sounded as formal as a soldier giving a report to his commander. He cleared his throat, which somehow made his actions even more awkward. "I see you like to talk to each other."

One of the soldiers who had turned her back on them turned around now just to give a most confused face to the pair of them.

The air around Talise stilled as she grasped for any words that could smooth this over. What would Marmie do? What would Wendy do?

Smile. Talise attempted a smile as sweet as Wendy's. Based on the sour looks the soldiers gave her, it hadn't been successful. She gave that up with a sigh. At this point, there was nothing to do but be honest.

"We want to get to know you better. We realize we've spent all this time trying to teach you, and we don't even know your names." She shrugged, grateful the words were coming more easily the longer she spoke. "We thought it might be easier to teach you if we spent more time getting to know you."

Now a smile came but this one wasn't as forced as the other. It wasn't as big or sweet as before, but it was genuine.

The soldiers seemed to be able to tell the difference.

One of them laughed at her. He was making fun, though not in an unkind way. "You realized we're actual people, have you?"

A blush warmed her cheeks, but there was no use denying the truth now. "Sorry it took so long. What are your names?"

After they all introduced themselves, the questions started to flow more naturally. The soldiers started taking on more detail around her. No longer were they moving props milling around the palace like mindless lumps.

Now they had life. One of them was excellent at Forces and had even beaten the emperor in a game once. Another of them liked to bake bread.

His parents owned a bakery in the Gate. He joined the army because his wife needed extra medical care, and it was easier to get in the Crown.

One soldier had just joined the army a few months earlier when she turned eighteen. She had dreams of guarding the palace by day and talking long walks in the garden at night.

Even their faces seemed clearer now that she took the time to look at them. One had a crooked tooth and bright eyes. One wore a uniform that looked even more crisp than Aaden's. One had a long scar on his neck, and the story of how she'd gotten it promised to be a good one.

Even Aaden warmed up the more they talked. His words were stilted at first, just like when he first started talking to Wendy and Claye. But the more they talked, the easier they fell into conversation.

The whole thing only lasted a few minutes. The soldiers had to leave to meet with General Gale. But once they left, Talise could tell her face was beaming.

# ELEVEN

**THE TRAINING HALL DIDN'T SEEM SO** ominous these days. Talise's heart didn't feel like crushing every time she walked through the doors. Now, almost every time she entered, she encountered a friendly face. She had started greeting the soldiers by name.

Many of them still didn't trust her. Gossip about her and Aaden's goal to get to know the soldiers had spread through the palace like wildfire. Some of them responded enthusiastically, excited to get to know the Master Shapers better.

Others still thought she and Aaden had no place being Master Shapers at all. Talise rested against the wall as their new class entered the room. It was Aaden's turn to head the lesson.

As the soldiers filed in, her expression grew darker. This was a squad they continually had trouble with. Every single one of the soldiers was firmly in the "don't trust the Master Shapers" camp. They had not only laughed at Talise and Aaden's attempts to befriend them, they also actively fought against their efforts.

So much for a good lesson.

To her dismay, the emperor entered the training room wearing an expression just short of a scowl. Aaden fidgeted at the sight of him. His jaw flexed, which made the bruise on his chin bulge. The bruise was almost faded now, but the memory had surely made an imprint.

Aaden bowed low, his voice the picture of respect. "What a great honor it is to have you here, Your Highness."

The emperor nodded at these words, momentarily appeased by Aaden's submission.

"I am here to check your progress. Fire Festival is approaching. I hope the soldiers will be ready to do a demonstration during the masquerade ball. The guests are expecting to see them shoot fire balls."

Talise's heart jumped into her throat. The emperor had implied they had until the festival to improve their leadership skills, but he had never mentioned a demonstration.

Letting her eyes travel the length of the room, the soldiers seemed just as surprised as her. Two looked frightened, one looked apprehensive, one looked annoyed. But the last soldier frightened her more than the others. The last soldier almost smiled beneath her haughty expression. She gave the tiniest glance to Talise, seeming intent on letting the mischief in her eyes shine through.

Great.

Sweat seeped through the skin of Talise's palms. The last thing she needed right now was trouble. The emperor seemed more eager every day to find fault with her methods. If she couldn't demonstrate some kind of progress during this lesson. No, best not to consider that.

Aaden nodded to the emperor. Though he maintained an air of calm, the pulsing vein at his throat told a different story. He was swallowing way too often. The trembling in his fingers wasn't obvious until he gestured toward the nearest soldier. Luckily, it was a small enough movement that no one would notice besides her.

"Gather the targets and place them along the back wall."

Talise admired how Aaden could speak in the face of fear without so much as a tremor in his voice. Their eyes met for a moment. Though they didn't speak, she hoped he would feel the encouragement in her glance.

Nearby, the soldier Aaden had spoken to glared at his request. His mouth shriveled up, and he made no attempt to hide his contempt from the emperor. Heavy footfalls sounded through the room as the soldier grudgingly complied with Aaden's order.

How would he like to be smacked upside the head? That might cure him of this unnecessary disdain. It would also probably undo all the work she had done to befriend the soldiers, but at the moment, she cared less and less.

A tiny quiver hung in Aaden's voice when he addressed the room again. His throat contracted like he was preparing to clear his throat, but he must have resisted the urge. "Before doing fire balls, try shaping a small fire over your palm. Just like we practiced a few days ago."

The soldier at the back of the room made a point of rolling her eyes. When that didn't illicit the reaction she wanted, she scoffed loudly.

One of the emperor's eyebrows cocked up slightly. His eyes drew away from the soldier and over to Aaden, perhaps awaiting his reaction.

Aaden wiped his palms on the side of his pants. He cleared his throat in two awkward coughs, apparently unable to resist the temptation a second time.

Smacking the soldiers upside the head seemed like a more viable option the longer Talise stood there. Aaden seemed to think the best option was to give a stern glare at the female soldier before he gestured at the soldiers to begin.

Most of them still struggled to shape a simple fire, even without throwing it. Were they doing it on purpose? Most students could shape all four elements when they finished the first five years of academy training. And yet these soldiers seemed to struggle with the simplest of tasks.

The female soldier at the back was the most concerning. She wore a blue-hemmed tunic, which meant she was a higher ranked guard. She'd already been trained by the other Master Shapers, yet still needed basic shape training. Why was shaping so difficult for her?

The emperor tapped his foot impatiently. As always, he was unhappy with their progress. He gave a pointed stare to both Talise and Aaden. Aaden responded by addressing the class again. He nearly growled as he told them to now throw fire balls at the targets.

His sudden intensity took the entire class off guard. A soldier in the front wore pinched lips as he turned toward the target. Another soldier had a shiver pass through his shoulders before he let out an audible gulp.

Guilt immediately lined Aaden's features, especially when he turned to Talise with an apologetic gleam in his eye. They'd both been trying to avoid this. They had decided to befriend the soldiers and gain their trust that way. Intimidation wasn't supposed to be the solution.

But when the soldiers aimed for the targets this time, all of them performed better than they ever had before.

The only one who neglected to produce a fire ball was, unsurprisingly, the female soldier in the back. Her haughty smirk was gone now. It had been replaced by a crease between her eyebrows that deepened as she began chewing her bottom lip.

She looked over her shoulder twice before holding her palm out in front of her. After staring at it for a moment, she began whispering and looking over her shoulder again, as if begging her hand to produce the fire needed.

Talise and Aaden shared another glance. His shoulders drooped as he stuffed his hands into his pockets. The guilt in his eyes was ever present, though the twitch in his lips made it clear he wasn't sure what to say.

"I'll talk to her," Talise whispered so the emperor wouldn't hear.

Aaden's chest heaved with a silent sigh as he bounced his head a little too enthusiastically in a nod.

When the soldier noticed Talise coming her way, she dropped her hand and pasted the haughty expression back onto her face. "This is a stupid exercise." She spit out each of her words like they tasted bitter in her mouth.

*She's just scared she's going to get in trouble,* she thought. *Remember what Marmie said. When people are scared, it often comes out as anger.* If she could be patient and gain the soldier's trust, she could be the leader she needed to be.

"Feel it in your heart first," Talise said, attempting a gentle smile.

The soldier responded by glaring through the side of her eye. "You're lucky to have a heart at all. No one should survive life in the *Storm*. They deserve to die."

The way her lip curled up when she said *Storm* sent ice prickling through Talise's veins. Her lips froze in place as she tried to formulate any sort of response that wasn't filled with wrath. People said awful things when they were scared or desperate. She knew that from living in the outer ring. But for someone to suggest that everyone in the Storm deserved to die?

*Breathe in. Breathe out. Don't say something you'll regret.* Talise pinched the side of her leg, forcing her focus on the pain and not on the anger.

The soldier's mouth twisted into a smile. Not only had she noticed the rush of anger Talise was battling, the soldier seemed to be enjoying it. In a scathing whisper, she added, "I hope your family members are all dead."

Talise took a breath so sharp, it sucked in her cheeks. Her fingers curled into fists without her permission.

And just like that, the emperor's silver and ivory tunic appeared at her side. How long had he been watching her? How much would he punish her if words like this went unchecked? This was about more than anger. It was about more than friendship or leadership too. If the emperor continued to disapprove her methods, he would do something about it. This was about survival now.

When Talise jabbed a finger under the soldier's collarbone, it seemed to be acting of its own accord. "You'll produce a fire ball and hit the target by the end of the lesson." Her voice was low and dangerous like a burning ember fighting to burst back into flames. "If you don't, you will suffer the consequences."

The soldier scoffed. Her head jerked to the side when the emperor shifted, and the barest hint of fear flickered through her eyes. The fear only lasted a moment. "What consequences? Are you going to make me sit in the corner?" The sing-song lilt of the soldier's voice begged a reaction.

Feeling the emperor's eyes on her, Talise jabbed the soldier again. "How does a night in the dungeon sound?" She spit the words out, surprised at how much wrath they held.

The soldier blinked. Then blinked again. "You can't...you..." The soldier stammered over her words as she glanced from the emperor back to Talise. Seeming to make a decision, the soldier lifted her chin. "You don't have the authority to do that."

This time, Talise turned her own mouth into a twisted smile. "Don't be so sure about that."

The soldier's eyes flitted back to the emperor's. When he remained silent, the soldier's throat contracted with a swallow. She looked at Talise once more, but soon her eyes fell, not exactly in a respectful way, but close enough.

"I'll do my best," she said, head pointed down. It wasn't until the soldier turned that a spark of guilt lit inside Talise.

The way the soldier's fingers shook as she glared at her palm. The way she glanced over her shoulder and kept chewing on her bottom lip.

That was because of Talise.

Talise pinched her leg again, eager to take back her threat. Perhaps it was better to walk away. Maybe it was better to let her thoughts clear before she faced the soldier again. When she took her first step backward, the emperor jerked his head side to side, refusing to let her leave. He pointed his chin toward the soldier, apparently urging her to watch.

But Talise didn't want to watch. That spark of guilt inside had already blossomed into a field of weeds that punctured through her insides. She'd been so eager to avoid threats. Anything to be different from the emperor. In the end, she had bowed to the pressure and acted just like him.

She was suddenly overcome with the desire to seek out Aaden. What would he think? Would he be impressed that she had frightened the soldier? Or would he be disappointed that she had been so cruel? For some reason, his opinion seemed to matter a lot more than the emperor's.

Just when the guilt exploded like the feathery seeds on a weed, the soldier produced a fire over her palm. The soldier let out a small shriek of delight before she clapped her other hand over her mouth.

After glancing back once more, the soldier focused her attention on the target. She reeled her arm back and punched it forward, which sent the fire ball arching through the air.

Talise expected another shriek delight when the fire ball hit the target. Instead, the soldier let out a breath of relief that made her shoulders sag. For a brief moment, she turned to the emperor, seeming to seek his approval.

He did not acknowledge the glance, instead he kept his eyes on Talise. As soon as the soldier turned her back on the emperor, he gave a simple nod to Talise.

He said nothing more as he left the room. The interaction left Talise at odds with herself. For possibly the first time ever, the emperor had not criticized her. Yet, the guilt crawling through her veins made the victory feel false.

Maybe she imagined it, but when she trudged back to the front of the room, the entire squad of soldiers seemed to hold their breaths as she passed. One of them definitely bowed to her.

It hadn't been her favorite method, but it had been effective. Maybe it was time to stop worrying so much. Maybe it was time to just accept the victory and do whatever it took to be a leader.

# TWELVE

**THE REMAINING DAYS LEADING TO** Fire Festival went by in a blur. Soon it arrived and Talise was still trying not to think about the demonstration the emperor expected that evening.

Immediately after lunch, she prepared to head down to the streets for the Fire Festival parade. When she pulled a fiery orange tunic over her trousers, she made sure to hide a dagger-clad belt underneath it. She'd been going around with the dagger a lot these days. After the attack on the palace, she just felt better having it close.

The streets were crowded by the time she left the palace. For some reason, she didn't want to think about how this was the first time in too long since she had been on a public road. She'd gotten a special pass, signed by Commander Blaise, that allowed her outside the palace grounds. But city soldiers wouldn't ask for passes today. They had too many other things to do during the parade.

She ran her thumb along the bottom hem of her orange tunic as she pushed through the crowds. The smell of hot candy made her mouth taste sweet. She eyed one of the popular confections. A hollow glass ball sat on a wooden stick. The design was reminiscent of something glass blown over a fire, a perfect treat for Fire Festival. The translucent candy had an orange hue. Just by the smell, she knew it had an extra large dose of cinnamon to make it taste like fire.

Her eyes lingered on the treat for another moment before she forced herself to look away. The streets were bathed in orange banners and streamers. Almost everyone in the milling crowd wore orange as well, from vibrant tangerine to understated copper. Everyone was eager to show their love of fire during Fire Festival, for fire brought the heat that melted the mountain snow. And the snow provided water for all of Kamdaria throughout the rest of the year.

Two old women nearly trampled over Talise as they held their heads close together sharing juicy gossip. A man called out the name Isla from across the street. His waving arms suggested he sought Talise's attention, which made her stomach flop. But it turned out, he was seeking his daughter, who was walking a few steps behind Talise.

Another smell lifted through the air. In a small market stall, a woman used fire shaping to roast a duck while her son turned the spit. A thick marmalade sauce coated the duck with orange peel shavings inside the sticky sauce. The woman's husband shaved the peels of oranges, tangerines, and mandarins into a bowl for another batch of sauce.

Licking her lips was inevitable. But when the small family offered to sell her some already cooked duck, Talise had to politely decline. She'd eaten breakfast in the palace and would have a grand dinner at the masquerade ball that evening. She didn't need anything in between. Besides, she didn't tend to carry around extra coins.

She marched down the street again, eyes narrowing to stay focused. Wendy and Claye came down hours ago to secure a good spot for the parade. Aaden offered to go down with her, but she told him she had one last thing to finish before she could go.

In truth, she didn't want him to get the wrong idea. He'd been getting bolder lately. He hadn't tried to kiss her yet, but everyone in the palace seemed to know exactly how much he wanted to. The latest palace gossip was all about whether she felt the same way. It probably would have been easier to tell if she knew herself.

Talise glanced over her shoulder to count the number of flags she'd passed. Wendy had said they would try to get a spot no more than seven flags past the palace gates. Since Talise had just passed her eleventh flag, she was beginning to think she should go back and look closer.

A sea of children appeared from nowhere, all screaming with delight as they charged for a nearby candy stall. They forced Talise forward with no time to check her surroundings. A moment later, someone tugged on her elbow freeing her from the mob.

Before she could rip her arm from the mysterious grasp, Aaden's voice lilted in from behind her. "We're back this way."

Talise's other hand flew up as she nervously tucked a strand of hair behind her ear. "I couldn't stop. The children, they..." For some reason, her stomach decided to start fluttering, making it difficult to form words.

The smile in Aaden's eyes didn't help at all. "I saw."

With his hand still on her elbow, he led her through the street. Even once Wendy and Claye came into view, he seemed to think it necessary to keep his hand over her elbow.

Wendy freed her from his grasp when she forced Talise onto a red and white quilt that had been spread onto the ground.

"We got this for you," Wendy said with bright red cheeks. She pushed a pasty topped with orange icing into Talise's hands. "Oh, and this!" Wendy retrieved a small bowl filled with diced cantaloupe, papaya, and mango.

Before Talise could pop one of the mango pieces into her mouth, Wendy bent at the waist and began digging around the quilt. Cloth napkins and empty tin cups went flying as she searched. "Claye, where are the meat skewers? You know, the ones with carrots and venison and that nice honey glaze?"

Claye didn't look up from the game of Forces he was playing with a stranger. He did chuckle slightly when he said, "You ate them all."

Wendy's cheeks turned even brighter red as her spine shot up straight. After biting her bottom lip, she let out a sigh. "Oh well, at least you have the pastry and fruit. I know I should have saved more for you, but..." She threw her hands into the air and spoke to the sky as if in prayer. "The food here is so good!"

Talise chuckled as she popped a second mango chunk into her mouth. "This is plenty, Wendy. Thank you."

Aaden folded his hands into his lap, somehow managing to look serious and ready for battle even though he sat cross-legged on a quilt. He stared across the street at a market stall that seemed to sell the exact meat skewers Wendy had mentioned earlier.

Even with his attention so diverted, his knee brushed against Talise's, which made her think he wasn't quite as distracted as he seemed. At least not by the market stall.

Claye dropped one of his Forces tablets onto the game board with a click. He grinned at his move and then turned to the others. "Talise, you have to tell me how you learned to shape all four elements before academy testing. My cousin is coming to the ball tonight. He has a daughter whose testing is coming up, and he's begging me for tips."

The stranger sitting across the Forces board from Claye looked up with mild interest but clearly not enough to say anything. He went back to the board right away.

Meanwhile, Talise's insides froze. She had difficulty chewing the pastry that had been soft only a moment ago. After some effort, she managed to choke out, "How did you know about that?"

Claye shrugged, his eyes on the board. "Everybody knows that."

The response didn't tell her anything because, as far as she knew, *nobody* knew about that. The only people in the room during her academy testing were her, Marmie, and the two guards.

Maybe the two guards had told other people, but what were the odds of Claye hearing about it from them and somehow connecting the event with her?

Wendy stopped brushing crumbs off the quilt and looked up with huge eyes. "*I* didn't know that." Her eyes opened even wider. "You could shape all four elements before academy testing? I couldn't even shape two."

"You didn't know that?" Claye rubbed the back of his neck as he glanced at Wendy. A nervous chuckle escaped him before he moved another tablet.

Talise pinned him with a questioning stare. He gulped and shifted in his seat, which only made her stare harder.

Her heart thrummed while a tingle of fear spread through her fingertips.

Claye leaned forward, suddenly over interested in the Forces board. He waved a distracted hand toward her. "Aaden told me about it. I thought everyone knew."

Talise whipped around to face Aaden, but his muscles seemed frozen in place as he looked at the market stall across the street. He seemed intent on pretending he hadn't even heard the conversation.

She wasn't fooled by his act. Her hands shook as she folded them tight. She blamed the bead of sweat dripping by her ear on the heat of the day, though deep down she knew that had nothing to do with it. "How did *you* know that?"

Her heart pulsed as she waited for his answer. Each beat felt like the sound of a gong reverberated through her veins.

Aaden finally turned, wearing an annoyingly convincing air of indifference. "I looked up your record from academy testing. They keep the testing records for every single student in the palace library."

"Why?" Talise took great care to keep her voice measured. And why was that information public anyway?

Aaden responded with a shrug. "It seems like a logical place to me. I guess they could keep the records in the treasury, but they aren't valuable. I mean, information is valuable, but not like jewels. And anyway, information is usually kept in a library."

Momentarily stunned by his masterful avoidance of her question, she blinked. Her elbow shot out to nudge him, which turned out more playful than she meant it. "I meant why did you look up my record?"

When her chest stilled in anticipation, she forced herself to suck in a breath. She wanted to let it out slowly, but that might make the others wonder why she cared so much. Instead, she did her best to breathe like normal. *In and out. Nice and slow.*

But really, *why* would Aaden look up her testing record? She'd been so slow to trust him because of his father's actions, so sure he couldn't be trusted. Had she been right about him all along?

He paused for a fraction, letting his eyes glance down the road before he spoke again. It wasn't enough to raise suspicion from anyone else, but now she knew him so well, she imagined he took the extra moment to formulate a lie.

"I wanted to know how someone from the Storm could shape. I thought maybe the guards who tested you left some notes or something."

Everything inside her felt like a thick-trunked tree just moments before an axe forced it to the ground. Her bones were cracking, her muscles were cracking. Her feelings. They were being ripped to tiny shreds that would scatter in the slightest wind. Torn and tattered, never to be repaired.

Her mind filled with all the moments they'd shared. Of how he'd helped her, of how she'd opened up to him. Of how he'd touched her. A shiver ran up her spine.

She wanted to take it all back now.

Could the others feel how the air around her shifted? Could they see how her body twitched, trying to get away from him without moving?

Aaden seemed to know. He *always* seemed to know. And she could see how his own face changed. The difference was subtle. The skin around his eyes softened. His chin tilted downward the tiniest bit. His shoulders rolled toward her.

He gazed into her eyes, but she knew he wasn't just looking. He was begging. He wanted her to know he had no nefarious purpose for looking up her testing record.

No matter how his eyes warmed her from the inside out, how could she believe that? What reason could he possibly have for looking up her testing record? And how, in all of Kamdaria, could it be innocent?

Claye seemed to think that was the perfect moment to change the subject entirely. While picking his teeth, he said, "Wendy told me the soldiers you've been training have to do a demonstration during the masquerade ball tonight."

The stranger sitting across from him didn't react to this statement. He probably worked in the palace too. Perhaps he worked with Claye in the gardens.

Talise forced her breaths to be even and slow. If she let herself worry too much, the others would notice eventually. She needed to tuck this information away and deal with it later. For now, she'd try to pretend it had never happened.

As Claye moved one of his blank tablets across the board, he pouted. "Why don't you ever tell me anything? You tell Wendy everything."

Talise took in another breath before she forced a friendly smirk on her face. With as much nonchalance as she could muster, she said, "Did you want to spend hours helping me pick out a mask and practice doing my hair for the ball? Because that's when I told Wendy."

Wendy giggled at the wrinkled face of disgust Claye made.

To Talise's surprise, the stranger spoke next. He raised one eyebrow. "Are you really doing a demonstration? My friend is a palace soldier, and she said only half of them can throw fire balls that actually hit the target."

More fear, cold and heavy, stabbed Talise in the gut. Her breath tried to shudder, but she controlled it at the last moment. She glanced at Aaden, who was inexplicably even closer than before. The same guilt laced his features that she felt in her own. At least in this they still shared common ground.

"Well *I* heard," Claye said, forcing all eyes on him, "that you two drastically changed your training tactics about a week ago. You went from trying to befriend the soldiers to barking off orders and doling out threats."

"We had to," Talise argued. But it sounded even weaker out loud than it did in her head. Could she ever get these emotions under control?

For the briefest moment, Wendy's lip curled. She hid the expression immediately and started scratching her nose. Perhaps she was trying to hide that her moment of disgust had ever appeared.

Talise folded her arms tighter around her chest, as if that could keep her calm. "The emperor expects a demonstration tonight, and intimidation was the only method that got us results. We're trying to protect them."

Wendy's head whipped around so fast it made her hair fly. "Trying to protect them? Or trying to protect yourselves?"

The moment the words left her, Wendy clapped a hand over her mouth, as if shocked they had escaped. Her eyebrows lowered apologetically. They dived down even deeper when Aaden glared at her.

"You don't know what it's like for her. You have no right to judge."

Talise touched his hand, which sucked the wrath out of his eyes in a single breath. When he turned to face her, Wendy seemed to be forgotten entirely.

Talise shook her head, staring at the ground. "No, Aaden. She's right. We should have tried harder to gain their trust. We should have done more to show we care about them."

When he spoke again, his words were just for her. They rang out soft and kind but no less piercing than they could be. "Then what are supposed to do? The demonstration is tonight, and they're not ready."

If an arrow had been shot in her heart it would have been less painful than this. A dozen different options fought for attention, but her mind kept coming back to one moment. One of the emperor's threats jangled through her, cutting away everything else.

*I'll send you back to the Storm.*

Her jaw clenched at the thought. She had won the competition, completed the trials. She succeeded in the battle against Kessoku, been officially named Master Shaper, and *still* he threatened to send her away.

If she couldn't prove her leadership skills, he'd never let her stay in the palace.

Gritting her teeth together, she said, "As soon as the parade is over, we'll gather the soldiers in the training hall. We'll practice through the entire masquerade ball if we have to. We'll find a way to make the demonstration succeed."

Wendy and Claye shared a skeptical glance before Claye went back to his Forces game. Wendy went back to fussing with the quilt. Only Aaden seemed to think her words had any truth to them. He nodded with a stoic face. Then, he squeezed her hand, which startled her because she had forgotten she was still touching him.

By the time the parade began, they were all laughing and talking like the conversation had never taken place. But as dancers glided through the streets with their fabric flames and orange streaked hair, Talise could only think of the demonstration.

And how she had to succeed.

# THIRTEEN

**SOLDIERS LINED THE WALLS OF THE** training hall, each wearing a unique version of a grimace. None of them had been happy about extra training. Over half of them verbally protested when Talise suggested they might have to train through the masquerade ball, not just before it.

The grumbling only increased in volume the longer they trained. And now the room was getting hot from all the fire balls.

Aaden fanned himself as he glared at the targets. Once the soldiers were told they couldn't go to the ball until they could hit the targets every time, their skills had greatly improved.

But it still wasn't good enough.

Talise lifted the hair away from her neck as she approached a nearby soldier. "You're so close." She attempted a smile, which felt ridiculous after trying to intimidate the same soldier the day before, but Wendy's earlier words rang in her ears.

She wouldn't turn to intimidation again no matter what. "Remember the fire ball is an extension of yourself. It's not the same as throwing a ball. It might help to pretend the fire ball is actually your arm and it can stretch all the way to the target."

The soldier huffed in response. He looked to the side, giving a longing glance at another soldier in the line. Talise started when she recognized the female soldier who had forced her to use intimidation in the first place.

The female soldier's hair was tied up in a messy braid. The heat from the room had turned her cheeks red.

The soldier in front of Talise seemed to think it was the most beautiful thing he had ever seen.

"Were you hoping to dance with her tonight?" Talise asked in a low voice.

The soldier jerked his face back toward the target but failed to keep his face free of emotion. He pushed a hand through his long hair and tried to laugh. "Tempest wouldn't want to dance with me. She's a blue guard, and I'm a yellow."

For some reason, this made Talise pause. She knew all about the different colors hemmed to the bottom of the guards' uniforms. The hierarchy was simple. Yellow was the lowest guard and silver was the highest, with red, green, blue, and orange in between.

But that hadn't surprised her. It had been the mention of the female soldier's name that made her stop. She'd made such an effort to learn names, but it hadn't occurred to her to learn the name of the soldier who defied her in front of the emperor.

But here was a person who clearly admired her. Tempest had a life. Tempest had friends and dreams. She had people who wanted to dance with her but who might be too afraid to ask.

It wouldn't do Talise any good to only befriend the soldiers who were kind to her. She couldn't only care for the ones who already respected her. She had to care for them all.

In that moment, something inside her changed. When she glanced down the training hall, she didn't see an obstacle. She didn't see people who stood in the way of her goals. For the first time, she saw people she needed to protect.

As their leader, this should have been her ultimate goal all along. Even gaining their trust wasn't as important.

If she wanted the best for them and clearly acted in their best interests, the trust would come.

Just as she tried to wrap her head around this new idea, the emperor waltzed into the room. Her insides flinched at the sight of him, but she willed herself to bow anyway.

"Guests have already started to arrive for the masquerade ball," the emperor said.

A collective groan of disappointment rippled out from the soldiers.

One sharp look from the emperor set the soldiers straight. He touched the edge of his crown, adjusting it slightly. The gesture seemed unfamiliar, but it was probably just because he wore a different crown tonight than he usually wore.

This one was polished silver with decorative tines that had small cutouts underneath them. He only wore this one on special occasions. The way he touched the crown again with an annoyed frown told Talise why. It required too much adjusting.

After getting the crown just where he wanted it, the emperor stood straight and looked past

Talise at the room. "I would like a preview of the demonstration I'll see tonight."

Aaden had appeared at Talise's side. His eyebrows rose, and she could tell his insides roiled with fear.

Her own insides sat still, as if waiting in anticipation. Her newest revelation had happened so recently, she hadn't had time to consider how it would affect her actions. But now was her chance.

She had finally realized the approach she should have taken all along. She didn't need to try to gain the soldiers' trust, she had to show them she would protect them.

A loose thread at the hem of her orange tunic provided the perfect distraction while she cleared her throat to speak. Even as she opened her mouth, she still had no idea what to say. How could she protect her soldiers? How could she demonstrate that she had their best interests at heart?

Her mind quickly passed over those questions and on to the next. What did they want?

Immediately, everything inside her changed again. Her breath halted as she stared at the room. The answer became clear even though it tore her apart.

At her side, Aaden seemed to think she had lost her tongue. When he opened his mouth to address the soldiers, she stopped him.

She cleared her throat once more, then she turned. Not to face the soldiers, but the emperor instead. "There will be no demonstration."

She expected Emperor Flarius to ridicule her, but he looked too shocked to react.

Before he could move, she went on. She let her voice ring loud and clear through the room. She wanted every soldier to hear. "My soldiers have worked hard and made great improvements. Three-fourths of them can now hit the targets with their fire balls. The rest are not far behind."

The emperor shook his head, the shock wearing off as he pinched his mouth into a knot. He glowered at her while a crease appeared between his eyes. "Did you say—"

"They have worked hard, and they deserve to enjoy the masquerade ball." It was bold of her to interrupt him. It was more than bold. It may have been suicidal.

His face continued to contort. It wasn't difficult to imagine the vicious words that threatened to spill from his lips. It was probably best to not give him the chance.

Talise turned to look out at the training hall. Her spine had never felt straighter. She feared the emperor's punishment, but something greater had taken hold of her now. It wasn't just about her anymore. She had soldiers to take care of.

"Soldiers," she said in a voice that surprised even herself. "Thank you for working so hard. We will continue your training in the morning. You are all dismissed." She couldn't help but smile when she saw how their faces lit up. With a rush of joy, she added, "Enjoy the ball."

Aaden stood by her side, but he added nothing to her words. His breathing had gotten shallow. Two different times, his eyes flicked to the emperor but he forced them back so he could stare ahead.

Talise didn't move. She smiled at her soldiers as they cleared out of the room. Tempest gave her the strangest look as she passed. Talise met it with a nod that she hoped conveyed the feeling she wanted.

She was on their side now. Even Tempest's.

Tempest nodded back. It seemed like understanding passed through her eyes before she left the room.

When the soldiers were gone, Talise didn't dare turn around to face the emperor. She could feel him standing in the same place he'd been the entire time, but she couldn't sense any of his other movements.

When he finally spoke, his voice was gruff. Deadly. "We will discuss this later."

His boots clomped as he marched out of the room. Her heart tightened with each of his steps. He hadn't punished her yet, but she knew it was only a delay, not a reprieve.

Punishment would come. Her heart fluttered as she imagined the possibilities. When she turned to Aaden, he said nothing. But he didn't have to either. His pursed lips and lowered eyebrows told her everything she needed to know.

He didn't approve.

# FOURTEEN

**TALISE'S FEET BARELY TOUCHED THE** floor as Wendy yanked her down the hall. Wendy had just put the finishing touches on Talise's hair less than a minute ago. Her short hair fell to its normal length just under her chin. But Wendy had gathered up the front pieces and pinned them with decorative combs and pearls in a look far too close to a tiara for Talise's taste.

But there hadn't been any time to argue about it.

"Hurry!" Wendy had a death grip on Talise's wrist as she flew down the hallway. "The First Melt is about to begin. If we miss it, Claye will never forgive us." Wendy brushed a hand over her gold-beaded bodice and put a hand to her mask to make sure it was still in place.

Moments later, they arrived just outside the ballroom. The sound of harps announced the beginning of the First Melt. Talise smoothed her own ivory dress as they walked through the doorway.

The embroidered blue flames on her tulle dress shimmered in the brightly lit ballroom. Tight in her hand, she held the silver and blue ombre mask Wendy had helped her pick out. With no time to put it on, she'd decided to secure it once they arrived in the ballroom. Her gown swished as Wendy helped them edge around the room until they could see better.

Through the crowd, Talise caught small glimpses of the First Melt. It was just a short play that recounted how Kamdar, the first emperor of Kamdaria, took a team of fire shapers to the top of the highest mountain. They melted the snow so it would trickle down the mountain and provide water to Kamdaria for the rest of the year. Even in the heat of summer, the highest mountain was a treacherous place. The First Melt recounted the epic tale of how Kamdar and his shapers fought wind, ice, and wild animals just so Kamdaria could have the water it needed.

In the Storm, children usually performed the play. They wore ill fitting homemade costumes and dirt smudges on their noses. Since no one in the Storm could shape, no one could move earth to act as the mountain. Wooden crates or overturned boats were used in their place. To add wind, a child who wore red weaved through the other children waving his arms wildly, usually while fighting a fit of giggles.

The First Melt at the palace had none of the same endearing characteristics. The play was serious with professional actors and extravagant costumes. The shapers who moved earth and wind were palace trained and performed their tasks with perfection.

When Wendy finally stopped, Talise gave a quick glance to the side to see where they had landed. The buffet tables stood only a few paces away. The smell of cinnamon baked apples and orange marmalade marinated chicken wafted in through her nose.

And Aaden was there.

He had been watching the First Melt, but once they stopped at his side, he glanced their way. His lips parted and his eyes went bug-eyed. His gaze brought a flutter through Talise's gut, but then he wouldn't stop staring.

He stared and stared while the tiniest smile appeared on his lips.

It was enough to make her squirm. "What is it?" she demanded. When his gaze lingered, she lightly slapped his upper arm with her cerulean paper fan.

"Her dress is stunning, isn't it?" Wendy said through a sigh.

"Not just her dress." One corner of Aaden's mouth turned up to a half grin that did all sorts of things to Talise's insides. The heat rising from her neck into her cheeks was probably turning into the brightest blush of all time.

She slapped him again, which brought a chuckle to his lips.

"Ooh look!" Wendy bounced on her toes as she pointed toward the middle of the ballroom. "Here comes Claye's part."

Aaden finally tore his gaze away from Talise, which would have been helpful except he also chose that moment to come to her side. Her insides bounced around as he took the mask from her hand and secured it in place on her head. Once finished, he stood close enough that their shoulders were touching.

Her breath caught in her throat. She had to spend an inordinate amount of time reminding herself he couldn't be trusted.

Still, no matter how she wanted to avoid him, she had a feeling he wouldn't let her be more than an arm's length away the entire evening. She'd have to find a way to get these emotions under control.

It didn't help that he wore a gorgeous gray suit made with such fine silk that it had a silvery sheen in just the right light. Under his high-collared suit jacket, a high-collared vermillion shirt peeked out with perfect frog closures holding it shut. The vermillion leaned toward orange just enough to be perfect for Fire Festival. But it also had enough red to make it stand out in the crowd. His mask was also vermillion with small gray accents.

And he must have trimmed his goatee recently because it looked neater, thicker, and, Kamdaria help her, more rugged than she'd ever seen it.

Yes, it would be hard to avoid him tonight.

When she finally managed to force her mind off Aaden, she focused on Claye. He wore a green mask to denote earth shaping was his primary. Even through the mask, Talise could see his eyes narrowed as he stared at the mountain of dirt in the middle of the ballroom.

Just as the actor portraying Kamdar reached the top of the mountain, Claye shaped the dirt under the actor's feet so it slipped away. The actor clutched his chest and cried out in mock fear. The dirt eventually stopped and held the actor in place halfway down the mountain.

Claye glanced over at Talise and the others before he waggled his eyebrows up and down with a triumphant smile. He had performed the dirt slipping trick perfectly. The rest of the First Melt had several shaping tricks thrown in. But Talise found herself pining for the version she had seen in the Storm.

When it ended, the crowd roared with applause while the actors took humble bows. And then the music began.

Not daring to give Aaden a chance to ask her to dance, Talise headed straight for the buffet tables and filled a plate high with the delectable food. Just as she suspected, Aaden was no more than a step behind her the entire time.

She ate until the seams in her dress were about to burst. And even then, she kept poking at the food on her plate, pretending she'd take another bite soon. This charade wouldn't last much longer. Wendy and Claye had long since finished their own food. They were busy dancing and laughing and enjoying every minute of the ball.

Aaden had delivered his empty plate to a waiter and stood patiently by Talise's side while she picked at her food. She needed another distraction immediately or he'd ask her to dance, and she might not be strong enough to refuse.

A nearby guest provided the perfect distraction. The guest wore a simple orange gown with a scoop neck and a feathery skirt. The girl tapped her toe just a fraction too fast to go in time with the music.

Her sequined mask hung funny on her nose like the tie had come loose, but she was too distracted to notice. The way she kept scratching a particular spot just under her chin proved she wasn't standing there waiting for a dance. She was nervous.

Even through the awkward hang of her mask, Talise could see how the girl blinked faster than normal. Every few seconds, her eyes would bounce from Emperor Flarius to General Gale and finally to Commander Blaise. All three of them were surrounded by a swarm of adoring guests who didn't look eager to leave.

Aaden cleared his throat. Before he could speak, Talise shoved her plate into his hands. "Give this to a waiter for me, will you?"

Rather than wait for his response, she walked over to the girl in orange. Even when Talise was at her side, her eyes kept shifting around the room from the emperor, the general, and then to the commander.

Apparently, Talise would have to do more than stand there to get the girl's attention. "Excuse me," she said in a polite voice.

The girl jumped and her mask slid off her face as the tie came completely undone. At once, Talise recognized her.

"Tempest?"

The soldier who had openly defied her only a week before stood blinking as she tried to catch her mask out of the air.

"Oh, Talise," she said when the mask was pinned securely between her fingers. "You startled me." Her lips pursed as her head gave a tiny shake. "I mean *Master Shaper* Talise."

"Are you all right?" Talise thought about patting the soldier on the arm the way Wendy probably would have done. But Tempest didn't seem like the kind of person who appreciated that sort of thing. Instead, Talise settled her face into an expression she hoped would convey the concern she felt. The mask covering her face probably didn't help.

Tempest did another quick head shake and started chewing on her bottom lip. Her focus had gone back to the head of the room.

Aaden appeared at Talise's side a moment later. The plate had apparently been delivered to a waiter.

"I'm fine," Tempest said when Talise didn't move. She managed a tight smile. "I'm just hoping someone will ask me to dance."

Talise raised one eyebrow and folded her arms in front of her chest. When Tempest's face fell, Talise knew her skepticism had been detected.

Her realization from earlier came back to her. If she wanted to be a true leader, she had to protect her soldiers.

She could walk away. She could pretend nothing was wrong and the soldier only wanted to dance. But the way Tempest kept looking around the room at the most influential men told Talise something bigger was happening.

This time, she did touch Tempest on the arm. In a gentle but firm voice, she said, "Is there anything we can do to help?"

For a moment, a huff of anger escaped Tempest. She tightened her fist around the sequined mask and started to shake her head. But then, she turned and looked at Talise with all new eyes.

It may have been her imagination, but Tempest seemed to remember how Talise had defied the emperor so the soldiers could enjoy the ball. If possible, Tempest probably still would have gone to the emperor or Commander Blaise first. But with no other options, she seemed to trust Talise enough to talk. "Can you find a way to talk to the emperor alone? I've been trying, but with so many people around it's impossible. But you two are Master Shapers. He might listen to you."

"Why do you need to talk to him?" Aaden's voice carried skepticism. Maybe even a hint of impatience.

Tempest must have been desperate. She stared at the two of them for a long moment before she leaned in with her head low. She glanced over her shoulder before lowering her voice to a whisper. "There are spies here tonight." She swallowed and leaned in closer. "Kessoku spies," she said significantly.

Kessoku? They weren't supposed to ever come back. Over two hundred of them had been killed when they tried to attack the palace. How had they been brave enough to try again? How had they gotten inside?

The question was answered in Talise's mind almost as soon as she asked it. Fire Festival. With so many people and so many festivities, it was impossible to keep track of everything. The members of Kessoku could have stolen an invitation from any number of people.

Talise opened her mouth, but Tempest didn't seem eager to allow an interruption.

She glanced over her shoulder again while fear flashed through her eyes. "I heard them talking in the hallway by the kitchens. As far as I know, they didn't hear or see me. I saw their masks, but I don't know why they're here. I just know they're looking for something. Or maybe some*one*."

Aaden's hand tightened around Talise's wrist in a firm grasp. He pulled her closer as he said, "You shouldn't have waited to tell anyone. Point them out immediately and we'll take care of them."

"No!" Tempest abandoned the whisper she'd been so careful to use earlier. She brought her hands to her mouth. Terror lined her brow with each jerk of her head. "They said if anyone discovers them, they'll attack the soldiers first. They don't care if they get caught and thrown into the dungeons. They're going to kill as many of us as they can before that happens."

"Then what do you expect us to do?" Aaden asked, pulling Talise even closer still.

Tempest started blinking furiously. She stuffed a fingernail into her mouth and began gnawing on it. Her shoulders shook as she glanced toward the emperor again.

By now, Aaden had his arm wrapped around Talise's waist. He held her tight with no indication of loosening his grip. Any other time she might have fought it. But right now, she was too busy thinking.

Her thumb traced over one of the fire flowers on her gown while she scanned the room. "The emperor will be too hard to get to. But we should be able to get Commander Blaise alone. We'll just tell him we have official Master Shaper business to discuss. He'll get the hint, don't you think?"

She intended to turn toward Aaden when she asked, but when she felt his chin brushing the top of her head, she thought better of it. "We just have to get across the ballroom without raising suspicion."

"Perfect." The first hint of agreement came through Aaden's voice. "We can dance over to him."

Talise's mouth wound into a tight knot. Before Aaden could steal her away, she gestured toward Wendy and Claye and begged Tempest to tell them everything including what the masks of the Kessoku spies looked like.

Only a moment later, Aaden swept her out to the middle of the ballroom. Apparently not even a pack of Kessoku spies could keep her from dancing tonight. She didn't dare protest for fear of raising suspicion.

But Aaden probably knew she wasn't a fan of this plan. He always knew.

He wasted no time in settling his hand as low on her back as possible. Soon his lips were at her ear, his breath kissing her skin.

He had something to say, and judging by how quickly he got into position, he had been waiting all night to say it.

# FIFTEEN

**MUSIC FILLED THE BALLROOM. AN** orange and purple clad musician plucked a steady melody on a koto string. Another musician in a rust colored suit beat a grounding rhythm on a taiko drum while the final musician in a marigold gown rang twinkling bells at spread out intervals.

The laughter and conversation of the room were drowned out by the lovely sound.

Yet, nothing could distract Talise from the heat of Aaden's skin against hers. Cheek to cheek, his lips practically touching her ear. Her heart felt like bursting from equal parts bliss and terror. It was all she could do to keep her feet dancing in time with the music.

When he finally spoke, it was obvious she'd been right. He had been waiting all night to say these words.

"You shouldn't have cancelled the demonstration."

She tried to pull away with a frustrated huff, but apparently, he wasn't done yet.

"You shouldn't have gone against the emperor like that. Especially not in front of the soldiers."

For a brief moment, she managed to pull away. "He wanted me to prove my leadership ability, didn't he? Maybe he should have been more careful what he asked for."

To her surprise, Aaden didn't offer a retort. He only tightened the grip of each of his hands. Neither the hand at her back nor the one around her fingers felt tight. They just felt warm and strong. Comforting.

"Why do you care anyway?" she asked. "It was obviously my idea. He won't punish you."

Aaden swallowed as he gazed into her eyes. Beneath his mask, she could see his scar from the Kessoku's sword. It had just finished scabbing. Now it stretched bright pink from his forehead to his chin. She almost laughed when she remembered how embarrassed he'd been about the injury. He'd worried it would make him less handsome.

Looking at him now, she could only conclude it did the opposite. The scar made him look strong and mysterious. It gave a glimpse of the pain Aaden had born throughout his life.

And since she knew the origin of the scar, it only deepened how attractive it made him. For he had earned that scar by protecting her. It was a symbol of the lengths he'd take to keep her safe.

Aaden didn't break his gaze. "You have no idea how the emperor will react." His grip tightened again. "I'm worried about you."

"Well, stop it." She would have stomped her foot if they hadn't been dancing.

"No."

She was the one to finally break the gaze. Inexplicably, she found herself resting her head on his shoulder. It was supposed to keep her from staring into his dangerous eyes. Instead, the increased physical contact only made her heart leap and twirl before it threatened to explode.

With him close, it was easy to assume he was telling the truth. She could see it in his eyes that he wanted what was best for her. At least it *seemed* like she could see it. He'd gotten that scar protecting her, and he stood up against the emperor for her, and he was always willing to help her when she needed it.

But then *why* had he looked up the record of her academy test?

Just when she was ready to throw caution to the wind and give in to him, he had to go and do that.

He leaned down, and his cheek met hers again. His breath warmed her ear. Her neck. It became difficult to dance. To breathe.

"Whatever he does, I'll help you. If he tries to lock you in the dungeons, I'll break you out."

"Aaden."

His voice grew more insistent. "If he strips your title and sends you back to the Storm, I'll come with you."

"Aaden." She straightened her elbow to force more space between them. "Don't worry about the emperor. I can handle him. We have more important things to worry about right now." She tipped her head toward Tempest, who was now whispering to Wendy and Claye on the other side of the ballroom.

He didn't seem eager to drop the conversation, but the song ended, and everyone stopped dancing. Talise pulled herself out of his arms. Since she didn't want to draw any unnecessary attention—and she assumed Aaden would protest their separation—she wrapped a hand over his bicep and allowed him to escort her toward Commander Blaise.

The commander's perfectly stoic face showed a trace of movement when the two of them approached. It was a fleeting expression, but for a moment, his eyes flicked to where Talise held Aaden's arm. She swore a smile tugged at the commander's lips for the slightest moment.

He still had a crowd surrounding him, but they dispersed quickly when Aaden asked for a private moment of his time. Talise wished they could take the conversation to another room, but that would certainly raise suspicion. The farthest corner would have to do. At least a few of the emperor's personal guards stood nearby.

"DON'T DO ANYTHING."

Commander Blaise's response stunned Talise into silence. She blinked twice and still couldn't imagine what to say. Looking at Aaden, it seemed words had failed him too.

"Maybe you didn't understand," Talise said giving her head a tiny shake.

"I understood perfectly." The commander held his back straight with one arm behind it in a fist. But the other hand he had casually placed over the decorative hilt of his sword.

"Kessoku is here looking for something." Aaden had explained this already, but when he said it this time, he put special significance on their name.

"Then we won't let them find it."

Talise swallowed. "What if they won't leave without it?"

The commander looked straight ahead. "Then we will wait until after the guests have left."

Aaden shifted on his feet before he answered. "If they get suspicious, Kessoku will attack the soldiers."

A vein on Commander Blaise's forehead pulsed. "It is their job to defend the palace. If they die, they will do it with honor."

Talise could feel Aaden's muscle go rigid under her hand. Her mouth had gone dry. This sounded like a horrible plan. "There has to be something we can do," Talise said through a croak.

At this, the commander's attention moved away from the ballroom. He glanced at her for the briefest moment before he looked to the side at one of the emperor's personal guards. "Perhaps," he said slowly, as if forming the thoughts as he went. "You should go to the treasury." He closed his mouth for a moment but then added. "To make sure it's secure."

Talise nodded and hoped her eyes didn't betray any mischief. If they went to the treasury, she and Aaden could create a new plan that didn't involve so much waiting. They could probably bring Wendy and Claye with them. More people working together would mean a higher chance of success.

Hopefully Aaden would agree they needed a new plan. Considering how he had yet to agree with his grandfather, she guessed he already felt the same as she did.

"I'll send a royal guard with you," Commander Blaise said.

The nearest guard immediately turned toward them, which suggested he had heard the entire conversation, even though he had acted like he didn't.

A tingle of anxiety ran through her. This could complicate her idea to make a new plan. She tried to give a defiant glare. "We're Master Shapers. We don't need a guard to babysit us."

The commander didn't acknowledge her words. He pointed toward her and Aaden and nodded once at the guard. And then he disappeared back to into the crowd where privacy was impossible.

Talise scowled at the guard. When she turned to Aaden, his eyes were alight with ideas. That made her grin. Soon they'd come up with another way to stop Kessoku. They just had to get Wendy and Claye and get to the treasury. With any luck, they could convince the guard to keep watch outside the door.

# SIXTEEN

**TALISE STARED AT THE BLANK WALL** in front of her while a weight dropped in her stomach.

"So, this is the treasury, huh?" Claye seemed to hold a laugh under his words. "It's a lot bigger than I expected."

"Oh hush, Claye." The sound of Wendy's fan hitting silk rang through the air. "What is it, Talise? What's wrong?"

Aaden was silent at her side. Then again, what was there to say?

Talise reached for the empty wall and traced her finger over a line of dust. "It's gone," she said in a whisper.

"What is? A crown or necklace or..." Wendy appeared at Talise's side, watching her trace the empty wall. Her eyebrows rose. "The emperor's family tree?"

Talise's veins throbbed. Her heart hammered as if trying to force its way out of her chest. How had Kessoku already succeeded? How had they gotten into the treasury without anyone knowing?

Or maybe someone did know. Maybe Kessoku had a palace worker on their side.

The thought made Talise's stomach churn.

Aaden glared at the wall, his hands stiffening into fists. "Then why are they still here? If they have the family tree, why don't they leave?"

"It's obvious, isn't it?" Claye perched himself on top of a table with gilded gold edges. "They're looking for an heir."

Talise jerked her head toward him. "There is no heir," she spat. All the emotions of the day were bubbling just under her skin and little by little she could feel herself falling apart at the seams.

"Well," Claye said giving a significant look to all of them.

Wendy jumped toward him, her eyes widening. "Did you find something?"

Claye grinned as he ran his fingers through his hair. He was enjoying this attention a little too much considering the safety of the empire was at stake. "I found something in the funeral accounts from after the Kessoku attack. You know how I've been studying them with Aaden? Apparently Princess Isla, the emperor's youngest child, was playing with a friend when the attack happened. They both died, but the body of the other little girl was never found."

Talise just managed to stop herself from hissing through her teeth. Clenching her jaw, she said, "How is that significant in any way? If the girl was a friend of the princess, then she had no royal blood."

Claye leaned forward, his eyebrows cocking upward. "Apparently, the friend looked a lot like Princess Isla. It's possible the girl was buried in her place and somehow the princess is still alive."

Talise scoffed loudly as she rolled her eyes. "While you're busy thinking up wild conspiracy theories, I'm going to come up with a plan."

Her gown swished as she began pacing the room. Every few seconds, she'd glance back at the empty space on the wall. They *had* to do something now. They couldn't let Kessoku leave the palace with the family tree.

Claye wrinkled his nose at Talise before he threw his hands into the air. "Fine, maybe there is no princess. Maybe they're here for Aaden."

Aaden had been stroking his goatee, apparently deep in thought. But at these words, he glanced up with mild interest. "Why would they want me?"

With a shrug, Claye said, "To recruit you. They killed all the other Master Shapers. Having you on their side would be a big blow to the emperor. Plus, we all know what your father did. They probably think you'd join them in a heartbeat."

The scar over Aaden's eye seemed to pulse as his eyebrows lowered in a glare. His voice was low, daring anyone to disagree. "My father doesn't work for Kessoku. He was only boasting. He was idiotic, but not treasonous."

"I'm just saying ..." Claye shook his head, apparently frustrated everyone had missed his point. "Kessoku probably assumes you're bitter about what happened."

Aaden jumped to Claye's side in one step. Even with Claye perched on the table, Aaden still seemed the taller one. He jabbed Claye in the chest with one finger. "My father destroyed my life the day he gave away those secrets. My great-great-grandfather was a Master Shaper, which means I should have automatically gotten a silver crescent moon on my ID card. But then my father made one mistake and my entire life was ruined."

His voice had started to crack. Each sentence came out shakier than the one before, but still he didn't stop. "He never even apologized to me. When my grandparents took me away, insisting they would raise me, my father didn't even put up a fight. So, forgive me, but I think I've earned the bitterness in my heart."

The others seemed affected by the shimmering in Aaden's eyes. Talise was not.

All the distrust she harbored for him came to a point. Ice curled through her veins as the room stilled. She let out a short laugh, hoping it sounded as cruel and cutting as she meant it. Her hands had formed fists and she could feel the blood rushing in and out of her fingers. Her skin felt hot, but her heart was ice.

"Every. Single. Person inside the emperor's mansion died that day." She took in a steadying breath, grateful the words sounded even crisper out loud than they had in her mind. "They're dead because of your father's actions. You spend so much time mourning how he ruined your life, but have you ever—even for one small moment—thought to feel a shred of guilt? Have you ever thought to mourn the *loss* of their lives instead of the destruction of your own?"

Her chest was falling in heavy panting breaths. The weight of her words filled in the room. She was glad for how she had spit the words out. Aaden deserved to feel ashamed.

It wasn't until this moment that she finally understood why it had been so difficult to trust him, but this was it. This was the heart of the issue. How could he dare to complain about his own life when so many were dead because of someone who shared his blood?

"You seem excessively passionate about the deaths of the royal family considering you never met them." Claye's voice cut through the air, and in a single moment, she could feel herself cracking from the inside out.

They knew.

Her breaths got shallow. Her heart seemed to stop.

They *knew*.

The royal family wasn't just the royal family. They were *her* family.

She could see it in each of their faces as understanding passed through them. Claye first. He knew before he spoke. His words and her reaction were only meant to provide confirmation.

Aaden was next. At first, he had been hurt. Truly ashamed after Talise's accusation but also offended that she could speak against him so openly. But then his eyebrows flicked up and his mouth dropped. Horror painted his features as the revelation hit him.

Wendy was last. She clapped a hand over her mouth as she let out a gasp. Then she stared at Talise as if trying to peel away the layers of their friendship, wondering how she could have missed something so huge. And then perhaps wondering how much more she didn't know.

Talise took a step back, grasping for the wall. Her legs had turned to the delicate hard candy children licked during the Fire Festival parade. And the candy had reached the point where its integrity failed. When it fell off the stick, and the children would pop it into their mouths, crunching it to dust before swallowing.

*Breathe.*

Twelve years of hiding. Two in the Storm and then ten in the academy. All those years she trained to ensure she'd become Master Shaper. It was the only way she could return without anyone batting an eye. Without raising suspicion. Twelve years of keeping her secret.

And it was all gone in a single breath.

Her legs still felt weak. She expected them to give out at any moment, but surprisingly, that wasn't the only thing she felt. Something inside her chest cracked under the pressure, but when it broke, she felt a wave of sweet relief.

Finally, she could share her secret. Finally, she had friends who could bear the burden with her. Years of loneliness and fear had wound her heart into a tight knot, but now it loosened.

For the first time in ten years, she felt like herself because she was finally surrounded by others who knew what that meant.

The relief was tangible, but it came at a cost. Because now that her secret was out, it meant any one of them could share it too.

She loved these people. Each of them had touched her heart in a different way. But as she looked at them, she couldn't help the fear that raced through her mind over and over, as steady as a drum. The question bit into her insides. No matter how she wanted to trust them, they now had a greater capacity to hurt her.

She couldn't help but wonder, *Which one of these three will betray me?*

# SEVENTEEN

**THE SOUND OF SHATTERING GLASS** and urgent screams came through the closed door of the treasury. Talise jumped at the noise. Even through the door, she could hear the guard outside drawing his sword.

"Kessoku," Wendy said breathlessly. "They must be attacking in the ballroom."

Talise didn't have the luxury to consider how her revealed secret would affect the rest of her life. All she could do now was hope her friends wouldn't betray her. She'd consider everything more carefully later.

Her feet sprang to the door. "We have to help them."

"No!" Both Aaden and Wendy shouted at the same time. He was too far away to reach her, but

Aaden held his hand out as if trying to hold her back.

"You have to stay here," Wendy said.

"Where it's *safe*." Aaden gave her a pointed stare. "Actually, we should get another guard outside the door."

"Or a dozen of them," Wendy offered.

Aaden nodded emphatically.

Talise glared at them both. "I'm not going to stand around while my soldiers are being killed." She threw the door open before either of them could protest.

"It's not like anyone else knows," Claye said from behind her. "What's the harm in her going?"

Wendy and Aaden were grumbling. Talise couldn't see what was happening behind her, but judging by the rustling of silk, she had a feeling Wendy was punching Claye in the arm.

Aaden caught up to her as she barreled down the hallway. "This is a bad idea," he said.

"If I put my life above that of my soldiers', what kind of a leader does that make me?"

"A living one." There was no humor in Aaden's response.

It didn't matter. He protested, but so far, he hadn't tried to stop her. He did the same thing he always did, which was to stand by her side. All those months of distrust and the truth had been there all along, demonstrated every day in each of his actions.

He was on her side.

She still had no idea why he had looked up her testing records, but maybe he had told the truth about that. Maybe he just wanted to understand how someone from the Storm could shape. Well, now he knew. She wasn't really from the Storm at all. She could shape four elements at academy testing because she'd been palace trained from birth.

No matter what his true intention, he was a part of her now. Not just in her life but in her heart.

The doors to the ballroom had guests spilling out, running for their lives. Talise had to elbow her way through the crowd just to gain entrance. By the time she pushed past them, she only had a split second to take in the scene of the ballroom.

Eleven of her soldiers in their masquerade clothes stood in a tight knot. A ring of fire burned around them like a rope. In a straight line in front of the soldiers, five men wielded swords. In a flash, they charged forward with their swords ready to pierce bone.

Time stood still as instinct took over. From the corner of her eye, Talise could see two large tubs from the First Melt sitting forgotten at the edge of the room. One of the tubs held the dirt that had represented the mountain. The other held water.

She levitated it into the air. There was no time to wonder if she could carry all the water on her own. No time to wonder if her plan would work.

She blasted the water at Kessoku. It formed a wall in front of them, which she froze to catch their swords inches before they met their targets. A few of the men fell when they collided with the ice wall. All of them stared at it in awe.

"Don't you touch my soldiers." She ripped off her heeled shoes and tossed them to the side. The water had splashed the fire rope before it turned to ice, which set her soldiers free.

The Kessoku's momentary shock had worn off. Apparently, they didn't think swords were necessary to attack. While their swords hung in the ice wall, two of the Kessoku spies blasted fire balls in her direction.

Using air, she blew them off course as she now marched toward them with bare feet. One member of Kessoku ripped off his masquerade mask, which prompted Talise to do the same. The added visibility would be imperative now.

With her eyes free of the mask, she noticed Aaden—also bare faced—charging at Kessoku with a sword in hand. She wondered where he had gotten the sword until she recognized the decorative hilt Commander Blaise had been stroking earlier.

The rest of the guards and soldiers were closing in on the spies now. These Kessoku had no chance for escape. That didn't seem to deter them in the slightest. They went back to their original goal of causing as much death and destruction before they got captured.

Waves of fire spread out through the room. Walls of wind knocked people and buffet tables to the ground. The dirt from the First Melt was begin flung straight into soldiers' mouths, forcing them to stop and cough it out.

Talise was momentarily distracted from her goal of catching them. Her sole focus was on protecting the others in the room. When the members of Kessoku had spread out through the room, she melted the ice wall and started shooting the water at any fire Kessoku tried to start.

Everything was happening so fast, the passage of time seemed to have suspended.

But whenever her water met a fire ball, part of the water evaporated. Talise didn't know how much time had passed, but at one point, she ran out of water.

When they kept shooting fire balls, she began shaping the punch that had spilled onto the floor near the overturned buffet tables. The sugar hung in the air when the fire balls evaporated the punch, making the room feel humid and sticky.

Aaden had his back to hers. He sliced his sword near anyone who attempted to harm her. With his other hand, he shaped fire balls, tornados of wind, and anything else to keep Kessoku away. He was trying to stop them too.

They all were.

But Kessoku fought with the ferocity of men who knew they had to fight or die. Talise slid dirt over the ground in a slithering snake. When it reached a Kessoku man, she entwined the earth snake around his ankle and yanked him to the ground.

She held him in place with the earth snake and then sent another one to entwine around his hands. Aaden was shouting behind her. Other members of Kessoku were near, but she couldn't think about them now.

Her only thought was on the man fighting against her earth snake. Two palace guards were headed toward him with chains clattering in their arms. She just had to hold the man a little longer.

The Kessoku man fought against her snakes, which sent a rip through her insides as if she had pulled a muscle.

They reached him at last and forced orange gloves over his hands before they slapped the chains around his wrists.

She let out a breath of relief as she turned to assess the rest of the room. Aaden had a Kessoku spy trapped under his sword. That meant there were only three Kessoku left. At that moment, she realized Aaden was shouting at her to duck. The command reached her at the same moment as she saw two arrows made of fire shooting straight toward her heart.

Her hands raised to do something, but she already knew it was too late. Suddenly, a great whooshing nearly caused her to lose her balance. But it hadn't been a wall of wind coming at her. Instead, it felt like the air was being pulled away.

When the fire arrows vanished from the lack of oxygen, Talise understood why. She had just enough time to give a grateful nod at Wendy before she turned her attention back to the fight.

Wendy's air shaping had given her another idea. Talise sent a tornado into the drapes that hung from the ceiling to the floor. Soon they were coming loose from their hangings. When the last curtain ring popped free, Talise sent air through the drape that sent it swooping through the air. It almost looked like her earth snake except much larger.

Shaping air, she wrapped the curtain around the remaining three members of Kessoku, holding them tightly in place.

174

Everyone else in the room let out a collective breath. It wasn't until that moment that she got a good look around the room.

Her soldiers had formed a circle around her. They seemed to be protecting her just as much as she had been protecting them. One soldier had drops of blood sliding down his cheek, but he looked okay. Tempest's feathery skirt had been sliced off from the knee down. Her legs were burned and blistered, but she was still walking.

One soldier had a dagger stuck in his shoulder, but he ignored it as he glared at each Kessoku spy in turn.

They were okay.

They'd all been injured and beaten in the fight, but her soldiers were okay. Her friends were okay. She was okay.

It seemed like a good moment to collapse and let out a fit of hysterical laughter. Anything to release some of the tension inside. She settled on grasping onto Aaden's arm. Her eyes ran over his body, checking that she hadn't missed any of his injuries.

From across the room, the emperor was just visible behind a wall of his royal guards. It was clear from the way he looked at her now that he'd been watching her carefully during the fight. From behind the guards, he did something she never expected.

He nodded to her solemnly, almost like a bow.

When she had defied him earlier and cancelled the demonstration, he showed nothing but pure rage. But now, everything had changed. He had seen how she fought for the soldiers. He had seen how she gained their respect.

His nod was more than just a simple gesture. It meant one thing.

She had earned her place as a leader.

"Are you okay?" Aaden was pulling the hair away from her neck, checking the spot where a dirt clod had slammed into her earlier.

"I'm fine. Stop fussing." She pushed him away as she moved through the ranks of the injured soldiers. Almost all the ones who had been attacked were her soldiers. Not just any soldiers, but the ones whose uniforms had a yellow hem. The ones she and Aaden had spent the last few months training. Even in their masquerade clothes, the attack had centered on them.

This was too perfect to be a coincidence.

The last traces of doubt left her mind. Kessoku had someone on the inside. How else could they have targeted those specific soldiers in a crowd of hundreds of guests?

Two soldiers whispered to each other from behind her. "The people know about Kessoku now. Even if we hide what happened to the Master Shapers, the people still know."

The second soldier whispered back. "That's the emperor's problem. He'll think of a way to regain the people's trust."

Talise glanced at Aaden, who had also heard the words. For a moment, she allowed herself to consider the fallout this attack would cause. But the moment ended, and she brushed those thoughts aside. There was work to be done.

A group of healers had entered the ballroom. Their hands were filled with medical supplies. As one of the least injured people in the room, Talise jogged toward the healers. She let them tuck supplies into her arms and nodded through their instructions on how to treat the lesser injuries.

The next several minutes were spent mopping up blood and shaping cold water over burns. Ointments and herbs were applied where needed. She took a moment to check on Wendy and Claye, eager to confirm they hadn't been too badly injured.

Wendy did have a few small scratches on the back of her hand. Claye had twisted his ankle early on in the fight, which left him relatively unscathed otherwise.

Once she was certain she had done all she could, she wandered over to Aaden, her feet seemingly acting without her control. So many questions lingered in his eyes.

Her heart tugged, knowing that now she could finally answer them.

Before she could disappear with him, a member of the royal guard approached her with a tiny bow. "Master Shaper Talise," she said, holding out a long roll of paper. "Emperor Flarius believes his family tree should not be returned to the treasury. He would like you to deliver it to his personal quarters off the throne room."

Talise responded with a bow of her own as she took the roll. The paper felt warm under her fingers.

Aaden didn't ask to accompany her. He just fell into step beside her as if that was where he belonged. And truthfully, she liked it that way.

# EIGHTEEN

**TALISE AND AADEN DIDN'T TALK MUCH** on their way to the emperor's quarters. Soldiers, palace workers, and lingering guests filled the hall. When they reached the fire orange door with the royal crest, Talise stuck her fingernail under a notch in the wall.

It took a moment to find the switch, but soon the lock clicked open. A hidden lock meant the door didn't need a key. It just needed someone who knew where the lock was hidden.

Aaden stared at the notch for a moment while the ghost of a memory passed through his eyes. He never had asked how she had gotten the door open when they'd snuck in to practice their ice and fire trees. Luckily, he'd been too distracted by the threat of getting caught.

Once inside the room, he took care to close the door tight while she placed the family tree on the wooden desk in the corner. She spread it open and traced a finger over the name on the tree that Kessoku was so desperate to find.

*Talise Isla Ember Ruemon.* Only her closest family members had ever known Isla wasn't originally her given name.

"Does the emperor know?" Aaden's first question came out the moment the door was secure.

She turned toward him and leaned against the desk. This first question was easy to answer, but it would bring a host of others. And some things she didn't know how to explain.

The words felt too tight in her throat. All she could manage was a nod.

Aaden's lip curled. "And still he treats you like... like filth?"

Her eyes averted. She rested a hand on the desk for support. Already the questions were heading in an uncomfortable direction. "He's trying to protect me. In his own way."

Aaden's jaw worked up and down while a dozen different responses seemed to dance on the tip of his tongue. In the end, he said nothing. He just shook his head and glared at the ground. "Does anyone else know?"

Talise bit into her bottom lip. She searched her dress for a piece of loose thread to fiddle with, but none appeared. Just as well. She couldn't avoid the truth now it was out. "Your grandfather knows." Her throat was tight, making it difficult to get the words out. "And a few of the royal guards. They've known since the beginning."

The brown in Aaden's eyes glowed as he blinked. He mouthed *my grandfather* while the shock seemed to settle on his insides. He shook his head again as if that would help everything make sense.

Her lip was getting raw under the weight of her teeth, but she couldn't bring herself to stop chewing. She wanted to answer his questions, but that didn't make it any easier. She hadn't faced these truths in a long time.

"Why does he treat you like that? The emperor." He returned to his earlier question apparently unable to move past it. He stared into her eyes, seeming to search for an answer that would made everything right.

Unfortunately, she didn't have one.

She shrugged, trying to move some of the weight off her heart. "He forced me to improve my sword skill because he wanted me to be able to protect myself... like the rest of my family couldn't."

Aaden curled his hand into a fist, once again mumbling silently as he glared at the emperor's desk. "And when he questioned your leadership?"

This question stung more than the others. The pain of it was still too fresh to ignore. Tears began swimming in her eyes. "He..." She swallowed. "He wants to make sure I'm ready to lead when the time comes."

One of Aaden's eyebrows raised as he folded his arms over his chest. "That's all?"

She let out a huff and squeezed the tears back inside. "Okay, and because he doesn't think I'm good enough. But it's more than that too."

Aaden peeled his arms apart as he leaned forward.

Talise reached for a piece of her hair, desperate for something to keep her fingers busy. Wrapping it around one finger, she said, "He's mad that I'm in this position in the first place. I was seventh born. I was his baby. He used to braid my hair and bring me ribbons. He taught me to play Forces. I was supposed to live a life of luxury with no need to understand the pain of grief and war. And now?"

"You're heir to the throne."

She ducked her head. Her hands fell and she kept folding and unfolding them in front of herself. "He blames himself, and he takes it out on me because he doesn't have my mother here to tell him when he's gone too far."

"Your mother?" Aaden's eyes narrowed as he said the words. She could see the way his muscles twitched as he tried to work out all the facts. He had known about Marmie for so long, it seemed as though it hadn't occurred to him until this moment that Marmie wasn't actually her mother at all.

His mouth hung open while his eyes narrowed more. She could practically see him putting the puzzle pieces together in his mind until finally he blinked. His eyes shot to hers. "Shyna, the empress's sister. Claye said she was mangled beyond recognition, that maybe it wasn't really her body that had been buried."

Talise nodded, unable to answer the question he suggested.

"Shyna was..." He paused, searching her eyes. When she didn't answer, he finally supplied the end of the sentence. "Marmie?"

Again, she could only respond with a nod.

Aaden shook his head, his eyes now wandering around the room. "She probably went by the name Shyna even in the Storm. It's such a common name, no one would suspect she was the empress's sister. Although, I'm guessing she went by a different last name than Malkshur."

"Mori." Talise shared the last name she had claimed for most of her life, one that Aaden had never heard. "Also a common name. Especially in the Storm."

At these words, Aaden froze. His face fell and the energy around him seem to burst. Suddenly, he was in front of her, grasping her shoulders. "He sent you to the Storm. The *Storm*."

"It was the safest place." The words tasted bitter in her mouth. "No one would ever think to look for me there."

Aaden squeezed her shoulders while his eyebrows knitted together. "You could have died."

She looked away. Her stomach squirmed with the same discomfort as it always did when she thought about the Storm too much. "I don't think he understands how bad it is there."

They both stood in silence for a few minutes. The air shifted while these new truths fell into place. They both needed a moment to consider how everything had changed.

"Talise."

He was still gripping her shoulders. He seemed to notice it at the same time she did, and his hands fell away in an instant. He gulped. He reached for one of the frog closures on his vermillion shirt and she wondered at how their roles had switched.

Now he was the one whose fingers needed something to fiddle with. He sucked in air, but when she thought he was going to speak, he let out a breath instead. When he finally spoke, his voice was almost a whisper. "Because of my father, your family is dead." He buried his head in his hands. "I'm so sorry."

"It wasn't your fault." It surprised her how quickly the words came. But not just the speed, her sincerity surprised her too. She had questioned the laws of Kamdaria before. Several times. Especially after living in the Storm. She questioned the separation of the rings and how punishments were bestowed onto children. And yet, deep down, a part of her had still believed in them.

These had been the laws of Kamdaria for centuries. They'd been put in place by the great Kamdar himself. Even as she questioned the laws, there had always been a part of her that assumed they were just. She always thought there must have been something she didn't understand because she was too young or naïve. Something the adults understood that would make the laws make sense.

Deep down, she had always believed if two people shared blood, then they also shared disposition. If a person committed a certain crime, then his child must also be capable of the same crime. It was why she feared Aaden so much.

But now it didn't matter what she had believed in the past. Aaden stood in front of her, burying his face in shame while his fingers dug into his hair. The normally combed strands now fell at odd angles since he kept tugging at them.

She pulled his hands away from his face. "It wasn't your fault, Aaden."

The agony in his eyes seemed to lift briefly at the mention of his name. His eyes were red as he looked at her. He closed the little distance that remained between them. Reaching up for her face, he seemed to take on a new purpose.

"I couldn't do anything to help you then, but I vow to you—"

She tried to stop him by shaking her head.

With a gentle tug, he held her head in place. His eyes conveyed even more determination than before. Stroking his thumb across her cheek, he said, "I vow I will do everything in my power to protect you now."

She didn't want him to think a promise like that was necessary. She had already forgiven him moments before. But the way he spoke those words with such conviction, did something to her that could never be undone.

He must have seen it in her eyes because the next thing she knew, he leaned down, and his lips met hers.

Heat seeped through her skin, sending shocks that enlivened every part of her body. The warmth she expected. She leaned into it, allowing herself the thrill she had denied for so long. But it was soft too.

His lips were the softest things she had ever felt, which didn't make any sense because the kisses were not gentle.

It wasn't enough. She wanted more. Needed more.

She pulled herself away from the desk, launching herself deeper in his arms. As close as they could be. Apparently, that still wasn't enough.

Aaden's hand trailed across her jaw, reaching under her ear and around her neck just so he could pull her closer still.

Before she could fully enjoy the moment, two pairs of hands gripped her arms and yanked her away. She blinked and three more pairs of arms struggled to rip Aaden away.

Her first wild thought was the emperor had seen them kissing and ordered his guards to pry them apart. But after her second blink, she recognized the faces of the men beating Aaden to the ground.

Kessoku.

The same five spies she had just caught back in the ballroom.

Aaden screamed out her name as she raised her hands to attack. The men clamped her arms to her side.

A cold, slithery voice slipped into her ear. "Hello, Princess," it said.

Something heavy hit her on the back of the head and then black curtained her vision while the world fell away.

## FIND OUT WHAT HAPPENS NEXT!

Talise's story continues in *Flame Crown*, The Elements of Kamdaria 4. Check out that beautiful cover!

*Kidnapped, imprisoned, and alone. But she isn't dead yet.*

DEAR READER,

Thank you so much for reading my book! If you liked it, please consider leaving a review on amazon or goodreads. Reviews are so helpful to me as an author, plus they help other readers know if a book is right for them.

To receive special offers, bonus content, and info on my new releases and other great reads, sign up for my email list! Psst, you'll get my short story collection for FREE. :)

**www.KayLMoody.com/gift**

Printed in Great Britain
by Amazon

43462986R00111